I0539207

A KISS AT
CHRISTMASTIDE

Christina McKnight

La Loma Elite Publishing

Copyright © 2016 by Christina McKnight

All rights reserved.
ISBN: 1-945089-06-7 (Paperback)
ISBN-13: 978-1-945089-06-0 (Paperback)
ISBN: 1-945089-05-9 (Electronic book)
ISBN-13: 978-1-945089-05-3 (Electronic book)

La Loma Elite Publishing

All rights reserved. No part of this publication may be
reproduced, distributed, or transmitted in any form or by
any means, including photocopying, recording, or other
electronic or mechanical methods, without the prior
written permission of the author, except in the case of brief
quotations embodied in critical reviews and certain other
noncommercial uses permitted by copyright law. For
permission requests, write to the author, addressed
"Attention: Permissions Coordinator," at the address
below.

ChristinaMcKnight.author@yahoo.com

Dedication

To Marc ~

Every story I write, every character I dream into reality within my pages, every creative idea that comes to mind has a bit of you in it. You are the essence of what goes into the perfect hero; compassion, caring, strength, integrity, faithfulness, loyalty, wit, intelligence, and above all else, endless, unconditional love for your family.

This book, the ones before it and the ones yet to be written, would never be possible without you by my side. You are the keeper of my hopes and dreams.

Thank you for allowing me the freedom to live my dream every single day!

Prologue

Lady Pippa Godfrey, the only daughter of the Duke and Duchess of Midcrest, sat in the front row of Lord and Lady Sheridan's musicale recital, awaiting her turn at the pianoforte. It was the final evening of entertainment, thrown in Lady Natalie's honor on the eve of her introduction to society. The room was crowded, overly hot, and the competing voices were deafening as Pippa waited for the next debutante to be called to the dais to apply her talents to her chosen instrument—some played the harpsichord or another stringed instrument, while others favored singing.

Pippa's fingers ached, and her head swam at the thought of standing before the large crowd—mostly strangers and only a few she could greet by name—and playing the complex piece her music tutor had requested she perform. It was then that she looked to her lap and realized her hands were clenched tightly, clutching the fabric of her gown, wrinkling the delicate material and causing pain in her fingers.

Forcing her eyes shut, Pippa took a calming breath and pleaded with her hands to release their death grip on her gown. The delicate material would likely be creased beyond her lady's maid's ability to straighten it. It was as if her hands had a mind of their own—and Pippa feared they'd take over once more when she settled behind the pianoforte.

She mustn't make a spectacle of herself before so many people—it certainly would not do to start her first London Season being the topic of gossip in every salon and ballroom.

A raspy female voice cleared not far from Pippa, the sound quieting the room instantly as everyone held their breaths.

When Pippa opened her eyes, Lady Natalie stood on the raised dais with a coy smile as she surveyed the audience. They were all staring at her as if she were about to announce something far grander than the next young girl to massacre a piece written by a great composer—or worse yet, pierce every eardrum in the room as she sang a note far too high. Her friend, Lady Natalie, was certainly at ease in her place as hostess and honoree of this grand three-day-long celebration.

In no way did she envy Natalie's effortless grace, for all Pippa wanted was for this evening—and her first Season—to be complete. For the moment, she'd settle for her time at the pianoforte to be over, for then she'd be allowed to depart the Sheridan townhouse for her own home in Mayfair. A few hours spent gowned in her night shift while reading a book by candlelight far into the morning hours, sounded much more pleasing to Pippa than standing before this crowd and announcing the piece that had been chosen for her to play while every set of eyes scrutinized her every move.

But Lady Natalie was her oldest and dearest friend.

Possibly her only friend.

And so, Pippa would smile, nod, and play the piano before giving a quick curtsey and allowing the next girl to take her moment in the spotlight.

It all sounded so very simple.

She'd been raised to do this exact thing, but no one could have expected the daughter of a duke to suffer from a shyness so severe she became short of breath and light-headed just pondering the notion of walking into a crowded ballroom. However, Pippa had pushed herself and fulfilled her daughterly obligations—entering a ballroom full of elegantly dressed women and stodgy men clustered in groups around the room. She'd even spotted several handsome men taking their turn around the dance floor. At first, her mother had allowed her to hide among the palms bordering the large room, but that hadn't lasted long. Men had approached her father and, eventually, placed their name on her dance card. And this evening had been no different—she garnered quite a bit of interest from eligible men, or so Lady Natalie had whispered to her several times. Her friend's words should have been a boon of sorts for them both. They'd dreamed for many years of entering society together and marrying titled, wealthy, handsome men—to the dismay and envious stares of all the other debutantes and their mothers.

But, while Natalie had whispered her shock over Pippa's popularity among the men, it sounded more of a hiss than a sigh of happiness. She'd put this behind her quickly the eve before.

This evening, as a new debutante and Lady Natalie's friend, Pippa was expected to play—and play well, as she and Natalie had shared an instructor since before their ninth summers.

Glancing at her mother who sat next to her, Pippa felt the urge to claim an illness and beg to be released from this obligation. But her mother's serene smile and encouraging nod made Pippa's erratic heartbeat slow. She prayed the sheen of perspiration on her forehead would dry before Natalie called on her. It would be embarrassing to have the light from the chandelier above reflect off her damp forehead.

Belatedly, Pippa realized her mother was nodding at her because her name *had* been called and the room was silently awaiting her arrival on the raised platform featuring a piano, harpsichord, and flute stand. There was also a small table with a dozen bells of varying sizes perched— oh, how Pippa wished she'd been assigned the bells. Not a soul would know if she shook one out of turn.

Except for Mr. Giles, Pippa's instructor, who stood not far from the stage, his hands clasped before him with a proud smile on his handsome face—staring directly at her as if she were the only woman in the room. It was his way of making his pupils feel safe and encouraged. Pippa was certain he'd cast the same intense, yet sensitive, look on Lady Natalie before she'd sang earlier in the evening.

"Go on, dear," her mother prodded. "It is your turn."

A lump formed in her throat and Pippa was glad she hadn't any vocal talent. It was unlikely any sound could maneuver past her blocked airway.

After a quick smile for her mother, Pippa glanced once more to Mr. Giles where he stood just off the dais— his shoulders stiff with pride at his accomplishments as an instructor. His hair was evenly combed into place, so much at odds with its haphazard messiness during their tutoring sessions. Pippa thought she much preferred the disorderly locks he favored in the schoolroom back in Somerset, where she and Natalie had grown up.

She stood, hoping her smile was one of beauty and not terror as she stepped toward Natalie, who'd barely had a free moment in the last few days to speak with Pippa. If they had been given a few minutes together, she would have told her friend that she dreaded playing before a crowd…that she'd be happy to sit with the second and third-Season young women and refrain from the piano. But the conversation hadn't happened, and Natalie was unaware that her friend wanted nothing less than to perform.

And it would speak negatively of Mr. Giles' tutelage if one of his students—the daughter of a duke, no less—were unable to play before a crowd. Pippa desperately wanted her tutor to be looked upon favorably by all of London society.

"Next to grace the stage, is Lady Pippa Godfrey, daughter of the esteemed Duke and Duchess of Midcrest—and my *dear* friend." Natalie gestured in Pippa's direction as an odd expression crossed her face. It was not one Pippa was familiar with; almost as if a bank of storm clouds moved across her friend's face. However, the look quickly passed, and Natalie's eyes sparkled once more. "Lady Pippa and I have been bosom friends since before we were allowed to touch a pianoforte. But since meeting, we've shared everything, including our music tutor, Mr. Giles, though I dare say Pippa is far closer to the man than my parents would ever allow. Her skills at the pianoforte certainly show the many hours of additional lessons she's endured."

Pippa's skin flared so hotly, she feared a candle had lit her gown—or her neatly pinned hair—ablaze.

Light female laughter and deep, manly chuckles filled the room, floating from the far back of the congregated crowd to the very front, where Pippa had sat back down with her parents.

She stole a glance to Mr. Giles who stood close to the edge of the dais, having only moments before congratulating another pupil on her success before the crowd. It was impossible to tell if his face flamed as hot as hers because he'd retreated a few steps into the shadows and was now backing out the terrace door.

A moment of confusion clouded her mind as the laughter dimmed and a light breeze assaulted her face—as if someone had opened a window to a gusty wind.

At her side, Pippa's mother fanned her face. Her wrist whipped to and fro, increasing as the room went silent.

Everything froze around her but her mother's thrashing fan.

The Duchess of Midcrest, her dear mother, who'd labored for over twenty years to rise above her merchant-class upbringing, would once again be embroiled in a scandal—all because of Pippa.

"Do you wish to depart?" her mother whispered.

"I did not..." Pippa stammered. "I would never..."

"I did not believe you had, my child." Her mother sought to soften the blow—something that society had done to the current Duchess of Midcrest a hundred times over. "However, that does not change the appearance of things, no matter what we say or do in this moment."

Pippa lifted her chin to keep her tears from streaming down her face.

"I do not understand why," Pippa said as she leaned in close to her mother to whisper. "Lady Natalie and I are such friends."

"Friendship and jealousy often hold hands so tightly that one cannot distinguish between the pair."

Pippa could not imagine why Lady Natalie would say such a thing—before the many people gathered at her parents' townhouse, amidst their first Season—and knowing her family sought a favorable match for her.

They'd shared a magical couple of days before the formal dinner introducing Natalie and then her ball the evening before. Pippa had danced every dance, her card filling quickly after entering the ballroom at the Sheridan townhouse. Lady Natalie had also danced almost every set and was escorted to dinner by the Marquis of Durshire, a wealthy, respected man whose handsomeness was legendary. Pippa and her family had stayed the night as the ball had lasted into the early morning hours. The girls had fallen into a deep slumber of exhaustion, their feet sore and their minds running wild at the grandness of their evening, only to sleep late into the day. When Pippa had awoken, Natalie was already surrounded by maids in preparation for this evening's entertainments. They hadn't time to speak on the matter of the recital.

But now, only a few short hours later, Pippa's dear friend had spoken aloud a comment that would ruin Pippa's chances of securing any type of promising match—and tarnish her family's name, once again.

Pippa wanted to ask why—what had she done to deserve such a comment before all these people?

She and Natalie had discussed their handsome music tutor in confidence, each laboring over the set of his strong jaw, the way his hair fell a bit too long in a very rakish way, and the muscles that lay under his loose linen shirt—certainly not obtained by musical endeavors.

Mr. Giles had removed himself entirely from the room by the time Pippa stared deeper into the shadows bordering the stage—leaving all eyes on Pippa with her back to the crowd. Lady Natalie smiled at her, awaiting her acceptance on the dais.

It was then that Pippa noticed Natalie's upturned smirk was not a smile at all—at least, not a smile one would bestow on a lifelong friend. And that smirk paired with the glare in her dear friend's eyes… Something drastic had changed since they'd journeyed to London a few days before to prepare for their Season.

Lady Natalie was issuing Pippa a challenge…much like a rival.

Pasting a serene smile on her face, Pippa squared her shoulders and stood to take her place behind the pianoforte.

She refused to allow her defeat to show—but certainly, Pippa had been bested, and by her bosom friend, no less. She only wished she'd known there was a battle at hand.

Chapter One

Somerset, England
December 1813

Lady Pippa stared into the open flames of the hearth—where a constant drizzle snaked down the chimney flue to pool behind the roaring fire—as the storm continued to rage outside. Her day—and night—had consisted of reading yet another book of her favorite holiday stories and watching the pooling water sizzle and dissipate as it approached the hot flames consuming the large logs. It had been her greatest tradition each year after arriving at her family's country manor, Helton House; hours turning into days as she re-read all her favorite holiday books.

The many hours were only interrupted by a footman entering to place another log on the fire. But it had been a long while since she'd bid the servant retire for the evening.

This night, Pippa had found it difficult—nearly impossible, actually—to concentrate on anything with the storm roaring outside. Especially since she knew she was essentially alone in the large house with all the servants having gone home before the storm, and the few that were in residence safely abed. Where Pippa should be herself. She pulled the blanket tighter around her legs as a draft moved through the room and chilled her exposed ankles. Glancing behind her, she expected to see Briars, her family butler, in the doorway, but the door was securely closed, and the aging servant was long asleep for the night.

A sharp light lit the room through the windows, the draperies still pinned back from where they'd been during the daylight hours. An onslaught of heavy rain pelted the thin windowpanes. Pippa regretted her request that the windows stay uncovered in case she spotted lights moving through the dark storm, signaling her parents' arrival.

But her wish of seeing anything through the angry storm declined as the torrential downpour continued hour after hour, making the local roads impassable by carriage. She only hoped the Duke and Duchess of Midcrest were wise enough to seek refuge from the drenching rains, lightning, and lashing wind on their way home from Bath.

Setting her book aside, Pippa removed her blanket and stood. Her toes touched the frigid floor as she moved quickly across the room to pull the drapes closed—locking out the sight of the lightning. With any luck, it would diminish the sound of the howling winds outside, as well.

She paused before the window, pulling the material back one last time, and stared out to the countryside surrounding her home. Though it was too dark to see anything, she'd spent the last eighteen years memorizing the landscape around Helton House: the rolling hills, the wooded area to the left of her property which everyone took as the border between her family and that of the Duke of Sheridan, Lady Natalie's father. In recent months, the trees had made a barrier that Pippa hadn't dared cross.

Their property even boasted a small pond that froze over during the colder months.

Unfortunately, this Yuletide celebration would not find her home surrounded by snow-covered hills or frost-kissed trees—or a pond frozen enough to walk upon. At this point, they'd be blessed to have dry, unmolded grain and hay to feed their livestock come spring. Pippa could only imagine the coming weeks of repairs the village would need due to leaking roofs and flooded dwellings.

Pippa sighed at the sight outside her manor—one that in no way resembled any Christmastide of the past. At this rate, she'd be lucky if her home didn't float away on a river created by the rain that had assaulted the area for almost a full day now—the temperature staying far above that of freezing.

Nothing about this year would be like the ones before, though the deplorable weather was not fully to blame. Pippa had sensed that things were not as they should be from the moment she'd received word that the Sheridans were hosting yet another three-day celebration to honor Natalie. This time, it was rumored that they'd announce her betrothal—to the son of a marquis, no less.

She should be happy for her dear friend—or, at least the girl she'd grown up with and thought of as a sister before Natalie had changed into a woman whom Pippa did not recognize. Her feelings toward the girl were petty, though grounded in truth. But wishing ill will on another was something Pippa found extreme discontent with.

In a huff, Pippa pulled the drapes shut, blocking out the rain and wind for good.

"I refuse to feel sorry for myself," she muttered, not for the first time since receiving the invitation to join Lady Natalie's holiday house party.

It was actually a blessing that her parents' carriage had been held up by the storm. They would likely insist on traveling the short mile to Lady Natalie's home to join in the revelry—to confirm that no animosity remained between the neighboring dukedoms.

No matter how much bitterness Pippa had locked within. Lady Natalie was to wed, and Pippa was alone—cast from society after the embarrassment of her first Season.

Even with all this, her mother staunchly believed that one could not find happiness and fulfillment in life if he or she cast negative thoughts and tidings toward another. A new reason to be thankful they were not here to witness her sulking about as if her prized gloves were missing or stained.

Picking up her book, Pippa fell back into the fluffy armchair she favored so. She tucked her feet under her and returned her blanket to ward off the growing cold in the room as the fire's intensity decreased. From her father's private study down the hall, eleven gongs could be heard, signaling the lateness of the night. For London, most would only be starting their evening by enjoying a meal with friends and acquaintances. But while in the country, Pippa delighted in being abed at sundown and rising when the sun made its next appearance on the horizon.

Early morning walks around the estate—from the house, out around the pond, and back through the stables to check on the animals—was a pastime she thoroughly found great pleasure in. She'd never thought she'd miss the freedom of her morning strolls after her introduction to society, but walking—other than in one of the many crowded parks in London proper—was frowned upon, especially without a proper chaperone. One could not think or ponder anything while being following by a maid.

The current storm had robbed Pippa of her morning out. As the day passed, she felt similar to the canaries women kept, a caged animal, longing to escape and roam.

Again, the storm was not fully to blame for her sense of overwhelming confinement.

It went far deeper than being trapped within her home during a nasty tempest.

The windowpane rattled as particularly heavy rain assaulted it once more followed by a thunderous racket. Lightning flared even through the drawn drapes. A door slamming somewhere deep within her home had her jumping with nervousness. The storm's intensity was only increasing as the night grew later.

She took a deep, calming breath before opening her book once more. Pippa started where she'd left off when she'd been distracted by the rain traveling into the chimney.

Had that been five minutes ago or five hours? Pippa had lost track of so many things of late.

Nothing contributed to her Christmastide cheer more than holiday tales of merriment—and she desperately hoped to repair her sullen mood. While in London, Pippa had discovered a small bookseller off Bond Street that was hidden from view down a narrow alley. Her mother had been more than agreeable to allow Pippa time to scour the shop while the duchess was fitted for new gowns. During one of her many visits, Pippa had found a thick tome full of ancient fables surrounding the winter months—not only tales from various Christian beliefs, but also pagan traditions, and even a few stories full of scary, hand-drawn images of ghosts and ghouls. Pippa had quickly flipped past those stories when she'd sat down to read shortly after her noonday meal, for they would only frighten her more with the storm raging so near.

Pippa was determined to banish her dour mood before her parents arrived—she may be a bit downcast, but she'd never allow that to ruin her mother's beloved holiday.

Turning the page, Pippa read yet another tale of the miracles of Christmastide, and love found during this magical time of year.

Her family property was rife with holly, and she'd had several groomsmen collect large sprigs for her just the previous day in preparation for decorating the house when her mother arrived home.

Pippa was vaguely familiar with the story of her parents' past. They'd found one another at a Christmastide celebration—and had fallen in love under a holly wreath set before a roaring fire.

Obviously, Lady Natalie had done her part to secure a match…while Pippa had buckled under the pressures of society and cut her first Season short in favor of an extended stay at her childhood home. If only Pippa would have read this book the previous year, maybe she could have secured a kiss before now—as the only men in residence at Helton House were her butler, several footmen, and the stable hands.

She pondered the notion of journeying to Lady Natalie's holiday party, hoping to land an eligible man worthy of her first kiss. But she pushed the thought aside when a loud bark of thunder ripped through the room.

The downpour was only swelling, along with the wind. The roads were flooded and impassable, even on horseback. And the hour was late.

Pippa was stuck.

At any other time, she would have been at peace with her fate, but not tonight. If an opening in the storm presented itself, she'd likely take the opportunity to flee—to London…possibly even Lady Natalie's celebration. Anywhere other than being here alone.

She should retire to her chambers, get some much-needed rest, and awake in a far more agreeable mood. Most things appeared brighter by morning light, or so her mother told her.

Shaking her head, Pippa cast a sidelong glance at the covered window before setting her book aside. Staying awake would not make the night pass any quicker, or the storm dissipate any sooner. She needed a good night's rest if her mother were to arrive in the morn, for holiday preparations would swiftly follow if she did.

Another loud clap of thunder shook the room—but it did not cease as the others had; instead, it continued steadily.

Surely the gates of hell were opening and releasing the ghouls and ghosts from their fiery pits. Pippa shouldn't have opened the book of Christmastide stories. She regretted the brief moment she'd spied the hand-drawn illustrations of creatures not of this realm.

It was then that a voice yelled above the storm, reaching her in the library.

It was not thunder at all, but someone pounding on her door.

She jumped to her feet and rushed toward the foyer to allow them entrance, grabbing her book and tucking it under her arm. Her parents, as radical as they were, must have thrown caution to the wind and traveled through the storm to see her. They were foolish, and their risk great; however, Pippa was overjoyed that they'd arrived.

Many things pushed to the forefront of her mind as she ran to open the door. She needed to call Cook to prepare them a meal, their bed should be prepped for them with hot coals to warm their linens, and the stable master need be awoken to tend to their horses.

Pippa was glad for the distraction from her previous melancholy mood.

Turning the lock, Pippa threw the door wide, a smile lighting her face for the first time that day—only to be faced with a stranger. On her doorstep was a man completely unknown to her, his hair matted and his clothing drenched and sticking to his thin frame.

"Is your master home?" he asked, removing his saturated hat from his balding head.

"I am Lady Pippa." She stared at the man intensely, waiting for him to state his business on Midcrest land and be gone.

"My lady," the man started over with his greeting, bowing. "I am repentant to awaken you, but my lord seeks shelter, and we have not passed an inn for many hours. The storm made it impossible for our carriage to continue on the main road."

Pippa remained silent as the man spoke, his body shuddering with cold as his saturated livery garb clung to him. She clutched the door with one hand to avoid it opening further in invitation, while her other arm pushed solidly against her side, keeping her book from falling to the floor.

"I fear our carriage is knee-deep in mud with the storm continuing to increase, and it has thrown a spoke." He looked at her expectantly, as if offering shelter was the only option for her. "My lord, the Earl of Maddox, requests refuge for the night if you will be so kind as to accept him."

"I…well…" Pippa's manners abandoned her at the same time she realized she was alone on the first floor of the house. "There is an inn only—"

A great wind hit Pippa, forcing her back, the door ripped from her hand. It slammed against the wall behind it. The sound echoed through the empty house as it collided with the tall walls of the foyer and rattled the chandelier as her loose tresses blocked her view. A moment of sheer panic seized her when her sight was taken from her.

Pippa pushed her hair away to continue with instructing the servant to the nearest inn. "Your lord will be far more comfortable…"

The wind whipped the last of her hair from her face to reveal not the servant from before, but a tall—very tall—broad-shouldered—very broad-shouldered—man. And that was all Pippa saw of him as her glance became locked on his chest. He was drenched, with his shirt plastered to his considerable width. It hadn't been the wind that had knocked the door from her hands and allowed the storm access to her home, but rather the man before her.

And he was fuming mad—his nostrils flared as water dripped from his hair and he stared at her pointedly—not bothering to mask his aggressive stance.

"Were you truly going to turn away a man in need of shelter?" his voice boomed.

Pippa gasped, taking yet another step back. She glanced quickly over her shoulder, hoping the noise had awoken one of her servants, abed on the third floor of the house. But none came running to aid her.

"I knew I was venturing into the depths of hell when I agreed to come all this way from London, but are manners not taught in the wilds of Somerset?" The man ran his hands down the front of his shirt, pushing the water from his body to pool on the floor beneath him. "My servants will need space in your stables. I thank you for"—he eyed her up and down before continuing—"your hospitality, my lady."

He bowed before Pippa with his last words, and his breath caressed her body, making her acutely aware of two things: *he* smelled heavily of spirits, and *she* was attired in a sheer nightshift that did not leave much to the imagination.

Chapter Two

Lucas Hartfeld, the Earl of Maddox, glared at the mousey woman before him, attempting to tamp down his irritation at and contempt for his situation—and the woman before him. His bloody carriage had broken down on possibly the worst stretch of their journey—long from any inn or tavern. He knew he should have denied his parents' request to join them for a Christmastide celebration in the country. It had been years since he'd ventured more than an hour's ride from London, and with good reason it seemed.

He'd never witnessed such a storm in London. He had never experienced so many miles between his next bottle of scotch and the last.

His head pounded from his previous night of drinking as he'd expected to sleep the entire ride to the country. However, the vicious storm raging outside his carriage had derailed his intentions. Now, he stood in an unfamiliar home, water dripping from his body, his hair likely askew, his Hessians overflowing with muck from his trek down this manor's long drive.

Lucas needed a bath and a warm bed.

A warm, *empty* bed—something he hadn't anticipated.

"Well?" Lucas asked as the woman continued to stare at him, her mouth gaping but no words leaving it. He knew she wasn't deaf for she'd responded to his valet's earlier request. For the first time, he noticed her hand clutching the neckline of her gown—a white, transparent, frilly nightshift—as if she were frightened of him.

Which was ludicrous. Women were *never* frightened of him. They were often infatuated, hung on his every word, and, on a few occasions, had been known to pay him a little more mind than was proper for a woman of the *ton*. But he'd never been...feared.

And what he saw in this girl's wide-eyed look was absolute terror—mixed with a bit of something else.

She wasn't even looking him in the eye. No, her stare had landed on his chest. One of his greatest assets, to be sure, from his hours spent at his boxing and fencing clubs—not to mention his nightly entertainments.

When her mouth finally snapped shut, and he saw her swallow, Lucas recognized the other emotion coursing through her—and he would be lying if he said it did not satisfy him greatly.

Lust. Pure, simple, uncomplicated lust.

Her expression, while flattering, was made all the more alluring by her demure, innocent appearance. The woman was certainly unfamiliar with men and was likely only just preparing for her first Season in London. If she sought to make a favorable match, she must learn to guard her baser instincts.

Lucas glanced over her shoulder, awaiting the appearance of her butler or another servant—or even the lord of the house, but none appeared. It was only the pair of them, alone but for his valet.

She dressed in a far from proper nightgown.

And he was sopping wet from the storm outside.

It had all the makings of one of those novels women in London seemed taken by in recent years. In fact, Lucas spied a book tucked under the woman's arm.

Had he walked directly into a sordid, risqué storybook?

His night was gaining absurdity as the hours passed; however, a bit more time before he arrived at the Duke of Sheridan's estate—and the woman his parents insisted he wed—was highly agreeable to him.

There was no hurry on Lucas's part to tie himself to a petty, self-centered, young debutante who'd demand he change his rakehell ways. It was what every woman did…and that sent him running for the safety of his club, whether it be White's or Gentleman Jackson's. He was whom he was, and that was not going to change anytime soon. Even the thought of being with one woman, day in and day out, had him questioning any need to marry at all.

"Shall I show myself to a room?" he asked.

Suddenly, the woman blinked, snapping from her daze. "You are drunk."

It wasn't a question but a statement. "Correction. I *was* drunk, but that was hours ago. Now, I have a raging headache, which you are not helping me alleviate with your uptight manners."

"Uptight?" she gasped. "Why, I never—"

"I am certain no person has ever told you to your face, but I assure you, your manners leave much to be desired."

Her hands moved to her hips, and she stared at him pointedly, letting the book beneath her arm fall forgotten to the floor as he prepared for a tongue-lashing he likely deserved.

The book landed with a thud, and the cover flopped open.

She broke her stare and dipped to retrieve her book, but Lucas was faster. He scooped it up and held it out to her. Water dripped from his arms with the movement.

When she didn't immediately take the tome, he tossed it on the table next to the door.

"Where were you headed?"

Lucas wasn't sure why his destination meant anything to her, but he gave in and answered. "A holiday party not far from here, but my carriage broke a wheel, and it is immovable in the storm."

"You cannot stay at Helton House," she huffed. "I can direct you and your servants to an inn that's not far from here. Only a short horseback ride over the next hill."

"You expect us to travel in this storm?" Lucas didn't bother concealing his exasperation at her denial of lodging. "We may very well be struck by lightning or drown in the torrential rains out there."

A smug grin lifted her lips, replacing her frown. "Oh, I am certain the lightning will find you as obtuse and bothersome as I do…and stay far away."

Lucas couldn't help but chuckle at her sharp wit. "Aw, I find we are at an impasse. May I at least coax from you the name of the woman who will so kindly give my servants and me shelter for the night?"

"I am Lady Pippa Godfrey, and you have arrived at the Duke of Midcrest's estate," she said. "But you shall not be finding shelter here."

"Is the duke available? I am certain he will have something different to say."

"It is the middle of the night, my lord." Her eyes narrowed at his forwardness. "He is most definitely not available. You may wait out front until he is and ask him then."

Could it be the woman was entirely alone in this large house?

No matter the commotion they'd made, no servants, nor her father, had come to investigate.

"May I offer another solution?" he asked, though her glare told him it would be met with the same reluctance as his last. However, he pushed forward. He was wet, disheveled, and freezing. "I will forget your less than customary greeting and our odd introduction, if you show me to a room—preferably one with a roaring fire and a suitable bed."

"May I offer yet another option for you to ponder?"

"Of course, Lady Pippa." He would entertain her womanly dramatics for only so long, though. "Please, share your idea."

"I sound the alarm, which will bring my servants running—and not only will you be thrown from this house, but the magistrate will be called."

A sweet, innocent smile settled on her rosy red lips, and she had the gall to bat her lashes at him.

"Or maybe I will catch my death of cold and perish before morning's light," he rebutted, realizing his irritation had fled, and he was openly enjoying their banter. "Please, let the magistrate know he can find my cold, deceased body over yonder in the shrubs."

A voice was cleared behind him, and Lucas turned to see his valet. "What, Charles?"

"The horses have been brought round, and a stable hand has prepared a few stalls for us to seek a bit of sleep in. I will assist you in the morning."

"Wait!" Lady Pippa squeaked as Charles gave his master a quick nod and departed for the stables. "You cannot—I have not—*humph*!"

Lucas took his time turning back to Lady Pippa, making sure his grin matched her smug smirk from a moment ago. "Thank you so much for your kind offer of shelter, my lady. Do you prefer I search the house for my own room?" He was staying, and no matter how much it irritated her, her own servants had outvoted Lady Pippa. "It is difficult to celebrate my victory with you glaring daggers at me."

Chapter Three

Pippa felt her face flush with indignation and fury at the nerve of this man…this *earl*. A gentleman of the *ton*, who should pride himself on his decorum and respect of the fairer sex, yet seemed to find fulfillment in leaving others speechless.

He was the one seeking shelter from her.

He was the one looking like a drowned rodent in her foyer.

He was the one being kicked from a home he was not wanted in.

Why did Pippa feel like the unwelcome party in this situation? As if he were the one with all the power; he who belonged while she was the interloper…nothing more than a trespasser in her own home.

Though, she knew, society dictated that she offer the man—no matter how irritating—shelter and a dry bed for the night.

"Lady Pippa," he said, his tone softening, and the laughter leaving his body. "I regret that we started on the wrong note. I am Lucas Hartfeld, the Earl of Maddox, and as I mentioned, my carriage was damaged beyond any repair attainable during this fierce storm. I throw myself at your mercy and request shelter…a bath and a warm meal."

She eyed him, watching for any indication that he mocked her with his tone or words. There was no teasing left in him. Before her stood a man drenched to the skin, his teeth starting to chatter from the cold.

"Very well, my lord." Pippa slid past him and retrieved her book. "I will ring for my butler, and he will show you to your room and make arrangements for a meal."

With a flourish meant to convey her curt dismissal of the man, Pippa pivoted toward the grand staircase, but her book hit his arm, casting it from her hands. It slid across the floor as the cover fell open and a slip of paper fluttered to the earl's feet.

Before Pippa could snatch the invitation to Lady Natalie's party, Lucas grabbed it. His brow rose in question as he read. "You are attending the Sheridan's holiday gathering?"

"No, I am not attending," Pippa confessed with a bit too much conviction, which only gained his inquisitive stare. "What I mean to say is that, yes, I was invited, but I am awaiting my parents' return from Bath. They may not arrive in time for us to attend." Too late, Pippa realized she'd told the man she was alone in her home without proper chaperones.

"Well, that is certainly a shame, because, other than my parents, you would be my only acquaintance." He handed the invitation back to her and walked farther into the foyer, inspecting a painting on the wall as he went—his Hessians sloshing with each waterlogged step. Pippa imagined it was fairly difficult to saunter when one was soaked to the core. "I guess I will manage, if this storm lets up and I'm able to continue my journey. How far is Lord and Lady Sheridan's estate?"

"Only a brisk, fifteen-minute walk through the cluster of trees bordering my home—to the north." It was the path she and Natalie had taken for years, having shared tutors and instructors, and also stealing away from home to spend time with one another. They'd been bosom friends—something Pippa had done her best to not dwell on since last Season and their unexpected falling-out. "Or a seven-minute coach ride."

He glanced over his shoulder to where she watched him. "Oh, then I dare say, if my wheel had lasted a bit longer, I would have made it. Pity."

"You are correct. But if you'd traveled any farther, you might not have seen my estate and sought refuge." Pippa was starting to warm to the idea of keeping one of Lady Natalie's guests from arriving on time for her celebration. If she could dampen Natalie's spirits, it would be well deserved for how she'd embarrassed Pippa. "I will call for Briars."

Pippa pulled quickly on the bell rope under the stairs…giving it an extra tug to make sure it awoke her servant.

"Please, do not let me keep you from your studies." He glanced at the book, still lying askew on the floor between them. "I can await your servant here and explain my predicament."

"You were not interrupting me," Pippa said. "I was merely reading for pleasure. Besides, it is long past my bedtime."

"Reading for pleasure?" he asked as if it were a foreign concept to him.

"Yes." She made no move to retrieve her book. "It is something I enjoy."

"There are many things I do for pleasure—and reading is not one of them," he mused, as if to himself. "But a bed...that is something that leads to great pleasure."

Pippa knew better than to gasp at his outrageous and highly scandalous remark. It was his aim to make her uncomfortable, though she knew not why.

"My lady?" a sleepy voice called from the hall off the foyer.

"Briars!" Pippa called, relief flooding her at the appearance of another person. It would put an end to her time alone with Lucas. "This is the Earl of Maddox, Lucas Hartfeld. His carriage broke a wheel on his way to the Sheridan estate. The storm is far too fierce for him to continue on tonight. Please, prepare a room, meal, and hot bath for him—in any order he requires."

"Certainly, Lady Pippa," Briars replied. "My apologies for the lateness of my arrival."

Pippa flipped her hand in dismissal as if to show his delayed assistance hadn't done any harm, and that she hadn't been highly uncomfortable during her time alone with the earl—yet, she knew she'd be unable to banish the sight of Lucas' wet, clinging linen shirt anytime soon. She only wondered what had become of his coat.

Briars cleared his throat. His eyes traveled from her head to her toes, silently insisting she do the same.

She'd completely forgotten her less than proper receiving attire due to Lucas's frustrating comments and demands for shelter. The man had a knack for distracting her.

A Kiss At Christmastide

"Yes, well, I will retire for the evening," Pippa said. "I bid you both a restful night."

She turned, with less flourish than earlier as it had only landed her in far deeper waters with the earl. She started toward the stairs—and the safety of her quarters.

"Lady Pippa?" Lucas called behind her. Lucas—she needed to remember that he was essentially a stranger, the Earl of Maddox, or "my lord." She turned to see he'd retrieved her forgotten book and held it out to her. "You will likely be missing this come morning."

He took the few steps to meet her, dissuading her from ignoring his offer of the book and fleeing to her chambers.

Pippa sighed and reached for the book.

She stiffened when their fingers touched—acutely aware of her nipples hardening beneath her nightshift.

At his inhaled breath, Pippa knew he'd noticed, too.

Quickly, she snatched the book and nodded in thanks before turning and rushing up the stairs; the book in one hand and her shift held high with the other. It would add insult to injury if she were to stumble before she was out of his sight.

"Sweet dreams, Lady Pippa."

The words floated after her until she reached the landing and turned down the corridor that led to her suite of rooms, a chuckle greeting her as she slammed the door behind her, throwing the bolt for safety's sake.

Chapter Four

Lucas stalked toward the aroma of eggs, ham, and warm bread, his anger from the night before continuing. The storm refused to break, his carriage was still thoroughly stuck on a muddied road, and his coachman hadn't any answers as to when they'd be able to depart Lady Pippa's home.

He was essentially at her mercy—something Lucas would normally enjoy. He appeared powerless at the hands of a innocently alluring woman, when truly, they both knew who held the power.

But the vixen he'd met the previous night would find little enjoyment knowing she could take the upper hand from him. Her meek demeanor was at odds with her saucy remarks.

There was no need to wander aimlessly as the breakfast room was not far from the kitchens, much like Lucas's family estate.

With no hesitation, Lucas entered the room, fully expecting to receive the full brunt of her ire for overpowering her wishes the night before. He would be livid if someone saw fit to disregard his commands and make themselves at home in *his* house. However, he'd had no other feasible options. Surely, Lady Pippa understood that.

Nevertheless, he entered the room, prepared for her pointed stare and demands that he and his servants leave posthaste.

The sight that greeted him was nothing he had expected.

Lady Pippa did not so much as look up from what occupied her or acknowledge his presence. It shouldn't vex him so—he was the unwelcome houseguest, after all, but Lucas had never been a man to be ignored—not by society, his servants, and, most assuredly, not by women.

"Good morn, Lady Pippa," Lucas ventured, as a servant stepped forward to hand him an empty plate to fill from the sideboard. "I hope you slept well." It was not an outright question, but certainly a comment she'd be forced to address unless she sought to further show the flaws in her upbringing and manners.

"My night was restful. Thank you for asking, my lord." She looked up as he arrived at the sideboard. He was forced to turn away from her to fill his plate or stand awkwardly and stare straight at her. "And yours?"

Lucas took in the mass quantities of food before him, shocked and a bit thrilled that the variety and selection before him were so vast—this far from *polite* society. There was more food here than he and Lady Pippa could eat in two days, and he assumed she'd already finished her meal.

"My room was warm, the bath very pleasing, and my bed suitable. If only the howling wind had subsided enough to allow a completely blissful sleep, it would have been appreciated, but that was not any fault of yours." He piled his plate high, feeling guilty if Lady Pippa's cook had prepared all this food only for him. "Thank you for asking, my lady."

The same servant as earlier snapped into action and pulled his chair out for him so he could sit directly across the table from Lady Pippa. He was able to see what occupied her as he sat. She held two needle-shaped instruments cumbersomely in her hands. The tips clinked as she seemed to knot some sort of yarn length. He'd never seen anything like it—his mother had never taken to such basic domestic responsibilities, regarding the mending and repairs of clothing as servant's work.

"What are you doing?" He stabbed a piece of meat and brought it to his mouth as he watched her work, fascinated by her swift movements.

"I am knitting a cap." Lady Pippa looked up at him as she continued to work as if her hands had done this job so many times they did not need her brain's directions. "Not all of us have the luxury of spending our time gallivanting about the countryside in search of merriment."

Her pointed words struck a nerve. "And is that your life's mission, my lady—to *knit* hideous caps for yourself?"

"These are not for me," she hissed, the insult in her voice clear.

"You mean to force those dreadful things on others?" Lucas looked at the small pile of green and red hats, complete with small balls attached to the tops—shocking him further, a few even had bells attached. "Tell me you are not requesting coin for them."

"Helping the less fortunate is a virtue that not all people possess, my lord. It does not make me think less of you that you do not understand this, though neither does it raise you in my estimation." Her stern expression had Lucas regretting his decision to leave his room.

"My apologies," he conceded. "It was not my intent to insult you. Your caps are lovely—very festive, indeed."

"They will keep the children in the village warm, which is all that matters to people who have so little."

If he'd wanted such a lecture, he would have attended a local vicarage to hear the many ways his life had gone awry. "That is very commendable of you," he said around another bite of food.

"Are you hungry, my lord?"

"I would not have gotten a plate if I weren't."

"It is only that your plate is so full it is overflowing on my mother's cherished table runner."

Lucas stared at his plate before him, noticing a small pile of eggs had, indeed, slid from his plate to land on the table when he'd knifed a large piece of ham. Hoping to avoid notice, he flicked his empty fork to push the escaped morsel back onto his plate.

"Has your coachman been able to fix your carriage?" she asked, focusing once again on her task. "While not as fierce, the storm has not subsided as much as I'd hoped."

"I am afraid not, though he will brave the weather and journey to town to see if the wheel is easy to repair or if a new one is available for purchase."

"Do you plan to ride ahead to the holiday party?" He noticed her fingers stilled for the first time when she asked the question, revealing her interest in his answer.

"It is highly risky to take a horse out in this weather," he said. "The chances of the beast twisting a hoof in a hole or throwing a shoe are greatly increased."

It was obvious by her nod that she already knew this, but she was giving him some sort of test—maybe to see if he'd risk his horse's safety, or assess how desperately he wished to arrive at the Sheridans' holiday party. Thankfully, for him—though likely not to Pippa's favor—Lucas was in no hurry to reach the duke's country estate. Namely, seeing his parents for the first time in almost two years was not something he was looking forward to. It would be the first holiday they had spent together since he was in knee britches and sent away to boarding school. Even now, Lucas only knew they'd summoned him for the specific purpose of introducing him to his intended bride—and shortly after, announcing their betrothal to all of society.

There was no other reason—and even now, he saw little need to meet his intended. They would meet eventually anyways…on their wedding day, certainly.

He and his parents had resided in London, moved within the same circles, for the past eight years, and never had their paths crossed…not in any ballroom or garden party or opera.

They avoided him, just as he avoided them. They had only seen one another a handful of times to discuss things of little import to Lucas.

It was a cycle they'd all become accustomed to. One he preferred as it left him to his own devices; however, Lucas was unsure what benefit it offered his parents, the Marquis and Marchioness of Bowmont.

"What are your plans for the day?" If he were stuck in her home, he at least hoped to find something to occupy his time—idleness was something he'd never favored. He was already tapping his foot rapidly against the floor, though he was thankful for the thick rug that muffled the sound. "I do not expect the storm to pass before supper, and my coachman may be in town most of the day hiring a blacksmith to repair my carriage."

Her brow pulled together at his question. "Today is the day my mother and I usually decorate for Yuletide. But, unfortunately, while the storm delivered you to my door, it has kept my parents away."

Lucas couldn't imagine why that pained her so, as he'd relish keeping his mother and father far from him.

"The holiday is, what…" Lucas searched his brain and counted the days. "…two days away?"

"Yes," she sighed. "Only two days, and we have much to do."

He glanced around the room, everything in its place. Much as the rest of the house he'd seen. Not a thing to be dusted or a table to be polished. Most of all, the house was startlingly empty, devoid of many servants—or possibly, they kept out of sight. He could not fathom what Lady Pippa had to prepare, especially if it were only she and her parents.

"Are you expecting more guests?" He would feel bad about intruding on a planned celebration with a completed guest list that didn't include him or room for an extra body. "I guess if the storm lets up a bit, I can depart."

"No, we are not expecting anyone else, but do not let me stop you from departing." Her smug smile returned, knowing she'd used his words against him once more. "But as much as I'd relish having my home back, my *manners* don't allow me to insist you leave. Did I pronounce that word correctly? M-a-n-n-e-r-s." Her smile faded as she looked at him with mock bafflement.

Lucas laughed, a deep reverberating sound. And it felt good, great if he were honest with himself. "Okay, you little minx, okay. I am sorry for my offensive mood last night. I was wet, cold, and inconvenienced."

Christina McKnight

"And I was not inconvenienced?" she asked innocently.

Lucas shook his head. "I will also admit that you were inconvenienced, and that it was my fault. Please, allow me to help with your decorating, at least during your mother's absence."

Setting her needles aside, Lady Pippa said, "That is not necessary, but thank you for your kind offer."

It was as if she sought any excuse to keep him at arm's length. She treated him no better than a stranger—which, by all accounts, he was. Then why did she seem so familiar to him? It was difficult to admit that they'd only met the previous night. Their back and forth was that of people who knew one another well and knew exactly the correct thing to say to gain the reaction desired.

Desire...

Most certainly he desired Lady Pippa. Who wouldn't? He watched her as she inspected the cloth under her empty plate, flicking a piece of lint from its surface. Her hair, while of the average shade of deep brown, shone like the sun. Her eyes—piercing and intense one moment, and soft, deep pools of warmth the next—confused him. Lucas was used to women who knew what they wanted and were not shy about demanding their due. It didn't matter if the woman was an actress who he'd sought out as a mistress, or a widow of the *ton*. Women did not play coy with him. Lucas hadn't the time or the energy. It was far easier to state your demands and expectations up front than to haggle over them once you'd become entangled with one another. Not that he had any intention of becoming the least bit entangled with Lady Pippa.

No, that hadn't crossed his mind once.

Not even at the sight of her hardening nipples through her sheer nightshift the previous night.

Lucas would perish before admitting he'd tossed and turned for hours after watching Lady Pippa flee up the stairs. And the rampant squall outside had nothing to do with his restlessness. No, a different storm altogether raged within.

Even more alluring than the sight of her rock-hard nipples were her shapely calves as she'd held her gown high and run up the stairs.

For the briefest of moments, Lucas had envisioned himself chasing her—all the way to her bedchambers.

Chapter Five

There wasn't a thing about her behavior Pippa found acceptable. She was being purposely disagreeable, combative, and not forthcoming. Yes, she was angry at Natalie for all she'd done during their first Season. Yes, she was envious that Natalie was having a grand holiday celebration to honor her—and would announce her betrothal come the New Year. And yes, Pippa was highly aware of her jealousy over the earl's intended destination. It maddened Pippa to no end that Natalie had ruined their lifelong friendship in such a disastrous way—and the reasoning behind it still eluded Pippa.

She'd written letters, had them hand-delivered by Midcrest livery. Only to have them returned unopened or no response given.

It was all so confusing—and utterly maddening.

Pippa was angry and hurt, and it had nothing to do with the Earl of Maddox. Yet, she'd seized every opportunity to take it out on him since his unexpected arrival.

Her actions should embarrass her, send her to her chambers in shame, but Pippa felt no such thing. It was likely due to Lucas's willingness to play along with her snide comments, giving back as much as he got. And partly because he had started the banter.

It was rare for her to find another so open and forward with their speech. Her time in London hadn't lasted long, and she'd met only a handful of people her age before escaping back to her country home. Neither of her parents had bothered to argue with her decision to forgo the rest of the Season. She wished they had—wished they'd demanded she stay at least until the end of the Season instead of allowing her to hide from sight after the callous way Natalie had announced Pippa's childish infatuation with Mr. Giles.

Pippa had enjoyed the same type of banter with Mr. Giles, though it had never turned to the suggestive. Though she and Mr. Giles had shared a competitive relationship. Her tutor had wagered Pippa could not master Latin in one year; Pippa had conquered it in less than six months. Pippa had gambled that her tutor could not play three instruments—a wind, a string, and a drum—at one time; Mr. Giles had managed four. Besides her parents and Natalie, Mr. Giles had been the only person she'd seen as a true friend.

And Natalie had taken that from her, along with their friendship. Most assuredly, Pippa knew her relationship with Mr. Giles was not to become a physical one, nor would it last into adulthood. But he was a kind man, a smart tutor, and witty…he was bloody witty.

A wit matched only by the Earl of Maddox. Lucas.

She'd told herself over and over the previous night that it was only his similarities to Mr. Giles that had sparked her interest. Their easy back and forth had captivated her most and kept her retorts coming, no matter the sting they likely left.

Belatedly, Pippa looked up to see Edmund, a stable hand she'd ask to assist her with hanging holly, watching her with his hand outstretched. He was waiting for her to hand him the next branch to be hung. How long had she been wrapped in her own musings?

"My apologies, Edmund," Pippa said, taking the wreath. "Thank you for agreeing to help me. I know decorating is likely not your favorite chore."

"Anything to bring me in from the wind and rain, m'lady."

"I cannot fault you for that." Pippa smiled at the young man. He'd grown up in the village between her family estate and Natalie's, attending a small schoolhouse Pippa's parents had funded. She also knew that he took all of his wages home to his family. He was a good servant, a loyal helper—as all who were staffed within this home were. "How is the foyer looking so far?"

"M'lady, I am not one to know, but I would say you will need one more branch over by the main door."

Pippa scrutinized the main area and saw that, indeed, the archway leading to the left did need a bit more cheer. "Yes, if you will move my ladder there…" She pointed to the passageway. "I will hang another while you collect more branches to start on the dining room."

"Yes, m'lady." He hurriedly moved the stool she was using as a ladder and departed to gather more branches.

She assessed the archway, deciding on the perfect placement for the holly. She knew the little metal pegs from previous years still lay hidden in the frame of the door, allowing for easy hanging each Christmastide season.

A Kiss At Christmastide

It would be a quiet celebration this year, so different from the last when Pippa had been overly excited about her presentation to society. She'd been a bottle of nerves with anticipation. At the moment, Lady Natalie was most likely organizing group games for her guests who'd arrived the day before for her three-day house party. The storm was keeping them inside, just as it was everyone at her home. However, Natalie enjoyed parlor games far more than the outdoors anyway, as she excelled at any competition. Pippa hadn't suspected there was any rivalry between her and her friend, but, apparently, she'd been wrong.

Pippa sighed and stepped onto the stool, deciding to hang the holly as it had been hung for many years prior. There was nothing to do but finish as much of the decorating as possible before her parents arrived—she sent a silent prayer upward that they reached her in time to spend the holiday together. Otherwise, they would be stuck at some unfamiliar inn, the earl would be safely at Natalie's, and Pippa would be alone.

As if on cue, the front door opened, the wind slamming it against its frame.

Pippa jumped with fright as her free hand grabbed for the wall closest to her to steady herself. It would be her luck to fall and turn her ankle.

She turned to see who'd entered, her hopes high once more that her family had arrived and she'd no longer be alone—however, it wasn't her parents, and Pippa was certainly not alone.

Lucas grasped the door and pushed it shut, fighting the storm for control as rain assaulted her entry floor for the second time.

His hair was, once again, sticking out in all directions, and his Hessians were covered in muck—reaching to his knees. He looked much like the night before, and she pitied his valet for the scrubbing of his boots and clothing that would be needed to remove the filth. Mud clung all the way to his shoulders—with a clot even clinging to his cheek.

Her urge was to laugh. However, he did not look pleased, and the fury in his expression matched his fierce stance. She did not discount his ability to battle the storm into submission, if only to suit his needs. He'd already won over her servants—just that morning at breakfast, her staff had been at his call, there to hand him an empty plate to fill and then removing it as soon as he'd taken his last bite. His coffee was refreshed without him signaling.

The earl's unknowing command over a room confused her—even more was the fact that he seemed oblivious to his power. Or he chose not to address it.

"My lord," Pippa snapped. "You are creating a mess! Kindly remove your soiled coat and boots before carrying the muck farther into my house. I do not relish my servants having to tidy up after my guests or me all day." She took a calming breath, remembering that she'd set about changing her attitude, for she was not to be labeled a scrooge during the holiday season. "My apologies. Do forgive my irksome comment. Where have you been?"

The earl shook his head, sending droplets of water to the floor around him, but he remained still so as not to track the mud farther into the house or damage any rugs. "I wanted to see the carriage for myself, which, as you can tell"—he held his arms wide to present himself—"did not go over well for me."

"Were you able to mend the conveyance?"

He shook his head once more, but this time, it wasn't to be rid of the water that dripped down his face. "No, in fact, I may have made matters worse. The storm is not letting up, and my carriage, along with the broken wheel, is two feet deep in muck. I will be lucky to have it extricated by spring."

Spring? He could not possibly think to stay at her home until spring!

"Do not look so frightened, my lady," he said. "As soon as the storm breaks, I will depart, even if my carriage is still unmovable. I will not overstay my welcome any longer than required."

"I was not worried about your stay," Pippa rushed. "It is only that I know you are missing all the festivities at the Sheridans' holiday party. I am sure you are anxious to arrive."

"It is only my parents there I know—and I am only attending at their request," he added as he removed his coat, careful to not shake it too much. "I have little interest in holiday festivities, I assure you."

"You do not enjoy the Christmastide season?" Pippa attempted to keep the shock from her voice.

"As difficult as it is to believe, no, I am not one for all the merriment and gift-giving."

"Someone who does not enjoy giving gifts?" It further stunned her.

"Oh, I enjoy giving gifts—as well as receiving them—however, that has not been the case for me in many years."

She sensed there was much behind his comment that he wasn't sharing, but before she could inquire, Edmund lumbered into the foyer, cutting off their conversation.

Pippa then changed the subject at hand. "My lord, I will have a bath sent to your room. A small meal will be served in an hour's time—we are not as formal, nor do we keep with London's hours here in the country."

When he nodded, Pippa turned back to her task, expecting Lucas to depart for his room and a clean change of clothes to make himself presentable for the evening meal.

"The foyer is looking very festive," he commented.

"Thank you." Pippa secured the greenery in her hands and made to turn toward him, but her shoulder bumped into Edmund, who'd moved to her side without her notice, and knocked her off balance. "Oh!"

Her arms waved wildly, attempting to regain her balance, but there was no helping it—she was falling, and fast. It would be more than merely her ankle that would be damaged when she eventually hit the ground.

When she landed, it was with a jolt, the wind knocked from her lungs, but no pain coursed through her body. Maybe she had gone into shock, pushed any pain from her mind? But, no, she looked up to see the wreath she'd hung far closer than she expected. Pippa turned her head slightly—Lucas's face was only a few inches from hers, his expression lit with concern.

Pippa's eyes were drawn to the symbol of Christmastide once more, and the many stories of her parents love founded during the holiday season flowed through her mind. Could that be her fate, as well? Possibly next Christmastide season?

The earl followed her gaze, a smile taking over his face. "Is this where we kiss, my lady?"

Her breath hitched as she longed to scream "yes," to take hold of his face between her palms and set her mouth against his.

Her first kiss—a kiss that would dictate her future.

Lucas was as handsome as they came, surely. Even now, her hand clutched his upper arm, muscular from years of…of what, she wasn't certain. He did not appear the type to embroil himself in manual labor, but she could not deny his strength, evident by his ability to cradle her in his arms as if she were as light as a feather.

"That would be highly improper. Besides, it's not mistletoe," Pippa said. As quickly as her thoughts of a kiss had sprung to mind—and the possibility of being wed before Lady Natalie—Lucas set her down, and the moment was gone. Made all the more final when Pippa realized the water and muck that had clung to him now also covered her—the soft peach of her gown marred by the mud from his clothes and the water still dripping from his hair.

Pippa cleared her throat, pushing her disappointment aside as they broke eye contact. "I will have a bath sent to your room immediately. Edmund," Pippa said, turning to her servant. His head was lowered in shame at his causation of her fall. "Will you handle the water?"

"That will not be necessary," Lucas cut off her request. "I only returned to beg a few tools from your stables. I may have a plan to release my carriage from the muck—but if all else fails, I need to have my trunk brought here."

"Very well. Instruct my staff to help in any manner necessary." The statement was unnecessary as all of her servants had taken to the lord immediately.

He stared at her, expecting her to say more, but Pippa only wanted him to go, especially after her fall and his offer of a kiss—if it could be considered an offer. It was more as if he were daring her to agree.

But she'd rebuffed his offer, and the only thing she'd received in return was a ruined dress.

Oh, for all that's holy above... Pippa realized she'd turned down his kiss—the kind of kiss that had led to her parent's great love.

She'd doomed herself; handed Natalie a victory of sorts, not that she'd admit to anyone that they were involved in any sort of competition.

"Are you unwell?" Lucas asked.

Pippa replaced her frown with a slight smile. "Of a sort. I must find my chambers and change. While I am very thankful for you catching me before I hit the ground, I now find myself coated in sludge and water from your time out in the storm. I will bid you good day, for now."

There was no time to await a reply. Pippa needed as much distance between them as she could obtain within the same house. Time to rid her mind of her scandalous thoughts regarding her houseguest, and Lucas being within reach was not helping. It seemed she was spending a great deal of time running away from things in her life. But the more she ran from the earl, the more she found herself in his presence.

Chapter Six

Lucas used a cotton towel to remove the excess water from his hair. He'd been a fool to go back out into the storm, but he'd seen little other option except to take Pippa in his arms once more and carry her straight to his guest chambers—and they would not have emerged until long after the holiday passed if he'd had his way. To keep his actions within his own control—a man could only be tempted so much before his gentlemanly resolve crashed and burned—he'd escaped the house for the stables with the guise of borrowing a tool. But he'd known there was no tool or device that could extricate his carriage until the storm passed and Mother Nature deemed it time.

Not long after, he'd tired of wandering about the stables. The servants—his included—began noting his attendance and asking if he needed anything. It was their kind way of asking why he was there—and when he planned to leave them to their chores without Lucas being underfoot.

He refused to return to the main house, and was more or less forced from the warmth of the stables, pushed into the storm once again. The temperatures had dropped, turning the rain to slush, making his trek about the property all the more harrowing. He'd lost his sense of adventure when he'd seen the pond in the distance, deciding the chance of seeing Pippa again was far more favorable than being outdoors.

Before too much time had passed, and too many long-buried memories assaulted him, Lucas returned to the main house and entered through the front door. He was thankful Lady Pippa was nowhere in sight. From the appearance of the room, she'd finished decorating and spreading holiday cheer here and had most likely moved on to another room. The scent of holly and evergreen branches permeated the room and, if Lucas were forced to admit it, it wasn't at all unwelcome. He quickly found his room and pulled the bell cord to have a bath prepared—maybe he would even find a bit of slumber before seeking his evening repast.

Lucas wanted to laugh at the insane thought—a nap?

Yes, he'd sought out his bed or that of others during the daylight hours, but never to sleep.

At this time of day, his evening was only just beginning; a night with his current ladylove, maybe the opera or a play, then he'd deposit her at her residence before seeking his gentlemen's club or a ball hosted by some lord whose name he would not remember past the front entrance.

He'd languished in his bath long past when the water turned cold, knowing he was avoiding something—or someone. But the rumbling in his stomach forced him out, and he quickly donned the clothes his valet had rescued for him from the carriage. His Hessians had been cleaned while he'd bathed, though Lucas hadn't heard his servant enter the room, nor return with the laundered boots.

The chambers he'd been given were adequate, if a little bare and feminine by his standards. The walls were constructed of a light-colored wood, and the covers—drapes, coverlet, and adornments—were all a sage green. The color was not the problem, however. Someone had taken it upon themselves to add frills to everything. Even the cloth covering the washstand was adorned with edgings. It was obviously the work of Lady Pippa. Upon closer inspection, he noted the intricate knitting stitch from the caps she'd been working on at breakfast—if there were such a thing as a preferred stitch for each knitter. Men commonly had preferred fencing patterns or boxing patterns, whether they favored aggressive jabs and punches as opposed to countering their opponent's moves. Women could not be so different in their hobby methodology.

There were two things fighting for control of his mind at the moment; food, and the lady of the house.

He was unsure which he wanted more.

Lady Pippa, while possessing a spirit unrivaled by all those he'd met before, had a kind and giving heart. She toiled away to knit caps for the village children. She'd welcomed him into her home—no matter how reluctantly—even though she could have sent him to sleep in the stables. She was not loud and demanding like the actresses he'd favored thus far in life. Nor was she petty and vain like many of the debutantes he'd met in the London ballrooms.

She carried herself like a country mouse—yet, he'd witnessed her hoyden side firsthand. The woman was quick-witted. It was no wonder her parents kept her hidden here in the country, for she'd attract every eligible—and not so eligible—man in town. Pippa was a rarity. Lucas had been among society enough to know that for a fact. The men would swarm and act the dandy to gain her attention, tripping over one another in pursuit of their prize.

However, that did not change the fact that she was the complete opposite of the women he normally pursued, the type of women he found alluring—that captured his full attention until they'd outlasted their usefulness to him.

Pippa was beautiful, in an unassuming, understated way—no coal lined her eyes, nor did she apply dyes to her full, pouty lips. She was a true beauty.

One that members of the *ton* would likely call a diamond of the first water, a rare jewel.

Could it be that he knew he was walking into a parson's noose when he arrived at Lady Natalie's country manor?

If Lucas had any sense at all, he'd set out for Lady Natalie's home on foot if need be to escape what he knew would result from his presence here—he would ruin Lady Pippa, as he'd ruined many things in his life. That was likely the reason his parents kept their distance, except in cases when they found their only surviving offspring useful. But they would discard him, send him back where he belonged, as soon as he'd fulfilled their needs—much like he'd done to those around him.

A vicious cycle…something Lucas was determined not to make Lady Pippa part of.

He hadn't been thinking when he'd asked her for a kiss, at least not with the head on his shoulders. The bell cord hung by the door, and Lucas knew he should pull it and request his meal in his room. Conversely, it had been hours since he'd seen Pippa, and he needed to see her as much as he required food.

Lucas pulled the drapes aside, hoping to see the storm had receded and the rain relented. To his utter surprise, the sun had set, and a purple haze sat on the horizon while the rain pelted the windowpanes. The raindrops etched a path down until they disappeared from sight. The wind still howled outside, and the trees in the distance waved wildly as if inviting him to enter the coming darkness and travel to them. They promised secrets far beyond his wildest dreams—but Lucas knew that calling was what had sent his life spiraling to its present condition. He'd answered the call of the darkness—ventured forth to explore its many secrets, all those years ago. He could still smell the air and hear the sound of rushing water in the distance as he'd snuck out through the kitchen of his family's country estate. It had been twilight, the same as now. He'd been ravenous for adventure, willing to brave the frigid frostiness of night to find it—if it ever truly existed.

Lucas hadn't known on that night that his younger brother—his only sibling—had followed him into the night. He'd been seven, and his brother only four. Lucas had spent that night vanquishing the pirates from his family's lands, hunting rare animals through the darkness, and rescuing the damsel in distress as light crested on the horizon. He'd returned and slipped into bed as his nursemaid had come to wake him and Randolph.

But Randolph's bed was empty.

He was nowhere to be found in the entire house— every servant and village member had searched for hours. They had combed every square inch of the estate until twilight landed once more, and Randolph was found—the life taken from his body as he lay almost frozen by the creek that meandered through their property. The exact spot Lucas had waged battle against his imaginary pirates during the night.

His parents had soon found his footprints leading back into the house after his night out.

They'd never forgiven him—sending him away the next week to be schooled far from the only home he'd ever known, devoid of any familial relationship.

Lucas had never ventured back to his family's country estate. Neither had his parents.

Pulling the drapes tight, he turned toward the door, banishing the thoughts from so long ago. With time, the images and hurt had dulled, though never completely fading. If he hadn't stolen a miniature portrait of Randolph before being sent away, Lucas would have long forgotten his brother's chubby cheeks and lopsided grin. He'd committed the image to memory as best he could, removing the picture it from its treasured spot when he felt the rendering fraying at the edges.

Lucas blamed himself for that night. He would never forgive himself. However, the sin of allowing his brother's appearance to fade completely from his memory would mean certain death for Lucas. When that time came, Lucas would be prepared for his life to end.

But until that day, he'd seek to distract himself as much as possible from his coming end. For he knew at some point, the sound of his sibling's light laughter would disappear altogether. His mind would eventually not be able to dredge up the long ago sound that had filled his life so utterly, and he'd be left a shell of a child after it was gone.

And that was when even the allure of London nightlife would cease to pull Lucas in and give him the illusion of comfort he'd convinced himself would see him through his life—until he and Randolph were reunited and he could kneel at his baby brother's feet and beg his forgiveness. Until then, London kept the loneliness at bay.

All this was made more real by his return to the country. It didn't matter that Somerset was far from his family estate—the calm, the quiet, the feeling of utter aloneness was the same. Lucas longed to surround himself with people once more. Maybe continuing to Lady Natalie's wasn't such a horrid idea. The holiday party was likely full to brimming with people, and distraction would be easily found.

London was his home—a place so teeming with life that Lucas could never get lost, nor be alone—but until he'd fulfilled this one obligation due his parents, he'd remain in the country.

He'd delayed in his room long enough. If he waited any longer, the nightly meal would be long over, and the servants in bed. That would leave him to a meal of day-old bread and cheese, much like the night before. After his morning meal of eggs and meat, Lucas knew Lady Pippa employed a wonderful cook, and he wasn't about to miss out. But when he arrived below, there was no one about. The dining parlor was empty; as was the room he'd broken his fast in.

A maid appeared, shuffling past him, increasing her pace. She appeared to be in a rush and wanted nothing more than to be away from Lucas—a stranger. He hadn't even a moment to ask after Lady Pippa's whereabouts as the maid kept her head lowered and continued on her way.

If all else failed, it would not be difficult to find the kitchens. Even now, the smells of food drifted his way—a mix of sugary goodness and savory meats.

His stomach growled again, protesting Lucas's slow progress toward the delicious aromas.

A part of Lucas wondered if the smells reaching him were those of the holiday season—sweet treats, doughy breads, and savory soups. He would not know since he hadn't spent a holiday with family since he'd actually had a family. His meals during the Christmastide season included anything his club offered; normally, a hearty repast of sautéed bird paired with wines, cheeses, and a spicy sauce that fit nothing but was well liked by club members.

Turning down one last hallway, he spotted the kitchen at the end. Candles blazed within, lighting the room as if a full staff of servants were busily at work—from the sound and smell of it, they were, though he didn't see a single person from his vantage point.

Curious as to what could possibly be the frenzy at such a time of night, Lucas entered the room—to find only Lady Pippa, elbow deep in flour with sugar crystals clinging to her deep brown hair.

Lucas didn't know if it was the sight of her, or the mess she'd created, that took his breath away. Yet, there he stood, only a foot into the room, his voice catching in his throat. He wanted to laugh. He wanted to remove each speck of sugar from her hair.

He wanted to take her in his arms once more.

Instead, he stood there as she kneaded a ball of dough, unaware of his presence.

Chapter Seven

Pippa huffed and blew a strand of hair from her eyes as she took in the chunky ball of dough before her. There was no use in kneading it anymore—it was ruined, nothing like the light, airy bread she and her mother made each year. She'd need to start over—for the third time—if she were to have time for the dough to rise, bake the loaves, and have them cooling before her parents' arrival. The thought of failing without her mother's guidance and helping hand wounded Pippa. Disappointing her mother was not something Pippa enjoyed doing. Cordelia Godfrey, the duchess, would never admit to being disappointed. She'd simply roll up her sleeves and show her only child how to make everything better.

But there is a time in a woman's life when she realizes she cannot depend on her mother to right every wrong. No, a woman must fend for herself, control her own life and destiny—or be left with nothing on the occasion her mother was not there to rescue her.

How was it possible that she'd stood in this very kitchen every Christmastide season and worked with her mother making all the pastries, breads, and mincemeat pies, and still she could not do it alone? Eighteen years of laughter, love, and baking together. Pippa had cherished the laughter far more than paying attention to the baking process, obvious from the utter disaster she'd made in the kitchen this night. Cook was likely to tan her hide when she arrived come morning—especially if Pippa had nothing to show for the disarray.

Maybe she should give up and simply clean the mess she'd made.

Pippa tossed the ruined dough on the table with the others and looked up, startled to see Lucas standing there, staring. He was outfitted in a freshly pressed shirt. His hair was damp from the bath she'd heard he'd requested over an hour before.

"My lord," Pippa greeted, rubbing her hands together to be rid of the flour. "I hope you enjoyed your bath."

"I did, thank you again." He nodded to her head. Pippa's hand darted to find her crown and brushed the sugar from the pie crust she'd attempted earlier from her hair. "I came in search of a meal, but I do not see anything edible at hand." He exaggerated his movements as he looked around the room.

Heat flooded her cheeks, and she wondered how long he'd been watching her.

"May I ask what you are doing?"

Pippa gave the room a desperate look before answering. "I was attempting to bake the pies, bread, and pastries for the holiday, but as you can see, I found little success."

"Why is your cook not here?"

Pippa sighed, resigned to admitting her failure. "Cook is given this night off each year to spend with her family—who live an hour's travel from the village—while my mother and I prepare things for our Christmas meal and bake sweet treats to deliver to the village on Christmas Day. I fear, this year, the villagers will have no gifts from us, and we will be left with only cheese and stale bread for our meal."

A look of concern, mixed with regret, crossed his face. The only signs he possessed any emotion other than anger and laughter. For the briefest of moments, he let his guard down long enough for her to glimpse something more within him.

"May I help with something?" He moved farther into the room, his posture serene. Another new development for him. "I cannot claim to have ever cooked a single meal, nor remember baking a pie. But if you can instruct me, maybe we can save your holiday feast together."

Pippa hadn't expected him to offer his assistance. However, she was grateful for it. "My mother normally does the instructing while I hurry about fetching things for her."

"Is there anything you do remember making from start to finish? We can start there." He removed his overcoat and slung it on a chair Pippa had used to reach a high shelf, then he rolled up his shirtsleeves. Instantly, she could imagine him on his own estate, no reluctance in rolling up his sleeves to help his tenants repair a roof or mend a gate. "If I can find something to snack on along the way, that would also suit."

"My apologies." Pippa rushed to the cupboard where Cook stored the bread, embarrassed that she hadn't thought to offer him a meal. After removing a half-loaf, she moved to the box that held ice and the meats and cheeses that were better kept cold. "I did not think to have a meal sent to your room. Please, take this." She handed him a plate of cold pheasant, cheese, and bread—all left from the previous night's meal.

"You need not fuss over me. I have had many years of practice taking care of myself."

"And yet you have never cooked a meal?" Pippa's brow raised in question.

"Very true, my lady," he said, inclining his head in thanks.

"I feel awful about your holiday plans going awry. I have spent the last two days feeling sorry for myself, when at least I am in my own home, surrounded by the familiar," Pippa said. "When you, my lord, are stuck in a strange house without even a single family member present. Yes, my Christmas is not as it has always been, but you, you are alone."

He chuckled, deeply, unlike the carefree sound she'd heard from him before. "I can assure you, this holiday is not so different from the many that came before it, my lady."

"You are alone at Christmastide often?" she asked before she could stop herself. "I do not mean to pry."

"Your question is not prying, and is something that all of London knows of me," he assured her, tearing a piece of bread from the loaf and popping it into his mouth. "My family…we are not close, and have not spent a holiday together since I was sent away to school when I was seven."

"I'm sorry—"

"Do not be," he cut her off. "It is best for all concerned."

59

He spoke about his family's distance as if it were commonplace; families spending special days apart—and a boy far from his family at such a young age. Pippa may be hurting from her parents' absence right now, but she'd enjoyed every holiday in the past with them.

"Do not look so dire, my lady." Lucas next selected a hunk of cheese and nibbled as he walked about the room, surveying the many bowls and discarded wrappings. "I was well cared for, the best schools, fine clothes, trips around England during breaks, and when I reached my majority, my own London townhouse. I was far more fortunate than many young lords."

Pippa sensed those things did not, indeed, make up for the lack of family, but rather that his insistence his youth was not a dismal time only covered up something far more damaging to him.

She would not pry—this was a time for celebration, not delving into Lucas's past—a past he obviously didn't want to discuss, and something Pippa had no right to know.

Besides, she had a holiday feast to save, even if the only people present to enjoy it were she and a man who'd been a complete stranger only the day before.

"Tell me, why are you so concerned with the villagers? Can they not make their own holiday treats?"

His lack of compassion for others was something Pippa did not understand. But from the softness in his voice, he didn't mean his question to be rude or make light of the villagers' circumstances—he'd obviously never been taught any differently than to treat the lower class as just that—below him. It was something made glaringly obvious to Pippa during her short time in London. Lords often treated the servants at balls as nothing. Those lords didn't so much as acknowledge their presence beyond taking a flute of champagne from their offered tray.

"My mother was once a villager here. Her father served my grandfather as a blacksmith," Pippa shared. Her family's past had made the gossip rags long before Pippa was born—and had, with time, faded. No one remembered the origins of the Duchess of Midcrest, something her mother disliked, as she was proud of her upbringing and her family. "My grandmother was a baker, teaching my mother all she knew." Pippa paused to cast a forlorn look about the kitchen. "Which it is evident, she did not pass on to me."

"Do not speak so harshly of yourself. Maybe with a few more years of practice, you will be as great as your grandmother is."

"Was."

"Was?" he asked. "I am sorry for your loss."

"Do not be, my grandparents passed when I was still in nappies." Pippa pushed his apology aside. "I do not remember them, except the smell of flour surrounding my grandmother."

A faraway look took over Lucas at her mention of relatives long gone from this earth.

Pippa hurried to the cold box once more, allowing him a spot of privacy to think through whatever had taken over his mind.

"What have you planned to attempt next, my lady?" Startled, she looked up to see him only a few paces behind her. "I am ready to assist you in any way. And if things do not fare well, you can lay the blame with me if anyone asks."

"How generous of you." Pippa laughed, retrieving a sack of minced meat Cook had prepared before leaving.

"We will start by filling the pie crusts I made earlier with mincemeat and putting them to bake."

"Lead away, my lady," he said, taking the sack from her hands.

"I am sorry the storm keeps you from Lady Natalie's holiday party. I am sure you will be sad to miss spending the time with your family for the first year in ages." His confession from earlier made all the more sense now that she knew he'd been kept from his family all these holiday seasons. He was likely angry the previous night due to that and not completely at the storm or having to leave London. "I do hope the storm lets up by morning, and all won't be completely lost."

He'd spotted her lopsided pie crusts on the side table and set the sack close. "If it does not, all will still not be lost."

Pippa wanted to ask what that comment meant, but his smile stopped her words. He was not overly concerned with missing Natalie's party, so she would not dwell on it, either. Surely, the Sheridans would not notice one guest missing. So what if that meant one less eligible man fawning over Natalie.

"What are you thinking about?"

"Nothing of import, why?"

"A smile, so smug, crossed your face, and I must admit that I find I must know what mischief was behind it." He untied the sack and peeked inside, avoiding staring at her. "Oh, this does, indeed, smell good. Do you think I can offer your cook a larger monthly allowance to come cook for me in London?"

"You would poach my staff?" The change of subject was preferable to admitting she'd found pleasure in knowing she'd kept a man, a lord ever so handsome, from attending her neighbors' holiday party. "I fear my entire family would follow her if she did accept your offer."

"And London would be a far better place for your arrival."

His comments, snide the previous night, shifted to almost endearing sentiments. That shocked Pippa. He was a different man than he'd appeared at first. No longer was he angry with biting remarks—and if she were pushed to admit it, she liked this side of him far more. Still, she could not forget that a certain darkness lived within him. She only hoped it didn't make another appearance during his stay.

"Now, tell me," he said as he stuck a fork in a jar of peach jam and brought it to his mouth. He paused, and his eyes drifted shut as he placed the sweet morsel on his tongue. He allowed a dramatic sigh to escape at the pleasure of the bite. "Heavens, my apologies. It is only that I've never tasted a jam so…" He tapped the utensil against his lips as he searched for the right word. Pippa didn't care what the correct word was—she couldn't look away from his mouth, a spot of peach still clinging to his bottom lip. His tongue swooped out and captured it. "Succulent."

"What?" Pippa drug her look from his smiling lips.

"Succulent, that is the term I would use to capture exactly how marvelous this jam is."

"I will let Cook know your pleasure at her canning."

"Oh, please do." He set the fork aside and stared. Pippa immediately busied herself filling the pie crusts with mincemeat from the sack. "As I was saying before heaven descended upon us and showed me what eternal salvation could be like—not that I am worthy of it—but, why are you not attending the holiday celebration? I must wager that the Sheridan chit is about your age, and you must have associated growing up being you live so close."

Pippa wanted nothing less than to answer his question. However, she thought that if she shared a bit with him, maybe he'd do the same. "Lady Natalie and I are friends—*were* friends. At least growing up. My estate and hers share a village. But…people grow and change. Sometimes, change cannot be explained."

"Was it you or she who changed?"

Pippa's brow knitted. The man was too perceptive for his own good. "Could it not be both of us?"

He pondered the thought by taking another heaping forkful of jam. "I suppose, yet it is my belief that people cannot change—they can only alter the way others view them."

"That is a very pessimistic way of looking at things."

"It is far better to think the worst and be surprised when it isn't as dire than to be taken aback when something negative happens." He leaned his hip against the countertop where she worked and crossed one leg over the other at his ankle. It was a relaxed pose—as if he felt completely at home in *her* home.

"That is very magnanimous of you, my lord." She finished the first pie and moved to the next. "But, have you stopped to think that maybe we have the same reasoning for not attending Lady Natalie's holiday party?"

"Oh, but I have every intention of attending. It is this storm that keeps me locked here in this primitive house with nothing but sugared jam as sustenance. I may very well perish from hunger before the rain and winds subside."

"That is rich, my lord!" Pippa flipped her spoon at him without thought, and a clump of meat hit his white linen shirt.

"And bereft of clean clothing, it would appear." He collected the meat before it dropped to the floor and popped it into his mouth. "If it isn't the storm, it is the tendency for flying morsels of food."

Pippa laughed, unable to hold it in any longer. "I am certain your valet is adept at fixing all the heinous things you do to your wardrobe, my lord."

"Lucas."

Pippa's eyes shot to his, not sure what she'd expected, but finding an openness altogether new. But hadn't she already thought of him as just plain Lucas?

"My name is Lucas. Please, call me such." He grabbed the filled pie and pulled it toward him, taking the flattened top crust pieces and laying them delicately over the meat in expert crisscross fashion, crimping the edges. "And I shall call you Pippa."

She wasn't sure if she was more shocked by her given name on his lips—lips that had been alluringly coated with jam only moments before—or the expert way he completed the pie top, far more uniform than Pippa had ever mastered. "Where did you learn to apply a pie lattice?"

"A lattice?" he asked, pinching the final spot on the crust.

"Yes, what you just did."

"Oh," he looked to her and back at the pie, taken aback by his own skill. "I do not ever remember learning, but I did spend much time in the kitchens when I was very young. Maybe, at some point, I helped our cook? Or, it is far more likely that I simply love eating pie."

"But you can't remember?"

A clouded expression settled on his face, and Pippa wished she hadn't pressed the matter.

"I fear much from my childhood is beyond my memory." He chuckled, but nothing in his confession was the least bit comical. "Now, where were we—"

A loud crash sounded, accompanied by breaking glass.

"What's that—"

Pippa wiped her floured hands on her gown without thinking and rushed from the kitchen. She could hear Lucas's heavy footsteps behind her as they both thundered down the hall toward the sound.

"Oh, no." Pippa sighed in distress when she saw the mess in the foyer. The garland she'd hung earlier had crashed to the floor, taking with it a small table that had been lined with miniature angel figurines. Pippa's own collection, given to her as gifts by her parents each Christmastide. She spotted one still intact and bent to retrieve it, only to have its delicate wing fall to the floor once more and shatter into a thousand tiny splinters.

There was nothing she could do, and it seemed that her holiday was going from bad to worse—her parents had yet to arrive, she'd been saddled with an unwanted houseguest, and, now, her collection was ruined. So many things taken from her in such a short time.

"My lady?" Lucas asked, his hand coming to rest on her shoulder. "Do not fret. I can help you right all of this."

Pippa swatted at the tears she hadn't realized she'd shed. "Pippa, call me Pippa. If you have seen me cry, then we are surely past formalities."

"Very well," he agreed. "Is there a broom nearby?"

"The butler's closet is just over there." Pippa pointed in the direction they'd come but kept her eyes on the destruction before her, not ready to face Lucas yet. "I will help you."

He was back with the broom quickly and began gathering all the tiny shards of glass into a pile. It was hard to imagine that all her years of gifts amounted to such a small pile.

Pippa allowed him to continue his sweeping as she grabbed the fallen greenery, assessing its damage. With a smidge of twisting, she righted the bent branches and looked around for her ladder or a stool. She should have made sure the branch was secured correctly earlier, though her fall and subsequent landing in Lucas's arms had entirely distracted her.

Certainly, all of this was his fault, though she kept that thought to herself.

"May I give you a boost?" His tendency to slip up behind her without making a sound unnerved her.

"My stool cannot be too far."

"Come now, I can hoist you up, and then we can return to the kitchen." His offer sent a shiver through her—to feel his touch once more… "I see the peg is still in place above the archway."

Pippa looked toward him, then back to the archway, clutching the branch close. Could she resist his newfound charm once again? It had been simple when he'd caught her earlier, his attitude had still rankled her—his forwardness and sarcastic comments kept her at bay. But those were gone now, replaced with sweet sentiments and visuals of him helping her in the kitchen.

He knelt before her and patted the step of sorts he'd made with his leg.

"I cannot balance on your leg—I may hurt you, or, worse yet, fall and injure myself!"

"I see your hesitation," he said, standing once more. "I will lift you then."

67

She moved before him, and he clasped her shoulders, turning her to face the archway, her back to him. Before she knew what his intent was, his strong, solid arms wrapped around her waist and he lifted her.

"My lord!" Pippa wiggled.

"My face is squarely in your skirts, Pippa. Call me Lucas." Indeed, her skirts did muffle his words, but the lighthearted nature of them showed through. "Now, will you hang that bloody thing already? I know I appear as strong as an ox, but I cannot hold you here all day."

Pippa giggled—something she hadn't done in many years.

She reached high, though the peg was still a few inches away. "A bit higher, Lucas, if you please."

She was unsure how he accomplished it, but he raised her the remaining distance, and she popped the branch back into place, giving it a small tug to make sure it would not fall again. "It is hung. You can return me to the ground."

"If I must," he teased. "I was beginning to enjoy the scent of your garments. Is that lavender?"

"Oh, you," Pippa squeaked and swatted at him. "Set me down before we topple over and we are both hurt."

"As you wish."

Pippa felt a moment of weightlessness, and she flipped about in his arms, now facing him as she slid to the floor—their bodies rubbing against one another in the most intimate and scandalous of ways.

Her breath hitched at the sensation that flooded her, pooling at her most guarded spot.

When the air finally left her lungs, it came in several quick pants.

Pippa blinked to bring her vision back into focus. Yet, all that did was have her breath catching once more because Lucas's face was a mere inch from hers.

And he was staring at her in the oddest of fashions.

Suddenly, Pippa noticed he held his breath, as well. It was as if they both feared breathing for it would end this moment, this highly unexpected moment.

"I think this should hold nicely," she said, breaking their stare.

Lucas looked up to assess her work, still holding her tightly to him.

She followed his gaze to avoid staring at his neck, which she knew led to his chest. His muscular, solid, capable chest.

"My lord," she whispered, and he turned his eyes to hers once more.

"Lucas."

"Lucas," she started again. "You may release me now."

"And if I refuse?"

"Then we shall be found in short order by my servants, in a position most scandalous."

"And we do not want that to happen?" This time, it was a question, not a statement. He was asking her if she wanted him to let her go—demanding she say the words aloud. But his words begged her to say no.

Pippa wanted nothing less than to be released. "Surely, the wisest decision would be that."

"Are you a wise woman, Pippa?" he asked, his breath fanning her face. "Because, I assure you, at this very moment, I do not feel like a wise man."

Chapter Eight

Lucas was flirting with danger. Every square inch of his body was on high alert—waiting. She need only say the word, or smile at him, and he'd pull her closer still. Bloody hell, if she so much as breathed, she'd likely set him ablaze where they stood—the heat being the undoing of them both.

But he was helpless to resist as she continued to stare. There were far worse places to be than lost in her deep, pooling eyes. For the second time, he sensed he was trapped in a story, a fairytale that he was hesitant to escape from.

"Ah, well." She glanced above them once more, to the mistletoe-laced garland. "It would be disastrous for me to deny you a kiss a second time, would it not?"

Her words were all the encouragement Lucas needed.

Slowly, giving her ample time to resist, he lowered this mouth to hers.

But she did not pull away as he set his lips to hers. Her luscious mouth tensed slightly at his touch but quickly relaxed and began to move with his. Their breaths melded together as if it were the most natural of occurrences, as if they did exactly this each day—every hour. Surprising him further, she increased her insistence, taking the lead from him as she parted her lips and ran her tongue across his lower one. Everything in his body hardened, and Lucas had a moment of hesitation, knowing their bodies were still pressed closely together—his erection unmistakable.

He was acting the randy schoolboy with his first bout of infatuation.

He slowed their kiss, allowing his hands to fall to his sides. Pippa was likely frightened by his actions.

Lucas should apologize, gather his belongings, and depart immediately.

The liberties he'd taken with Lady Pippa were unforgivable—and if he stayed, he knew he'd only insist on more.

"My lady," Lucas said as he pulled back. "I—"

"It is Pippa," she corrected, setting her lips to his once more.

Lucas gave in, allowing his hands their freedom, and they instantly wrapped around her once more to cup the round swells of her backside.

He released her lips and trailed light kisses along her jawline and up to her earlobe, taking it into his mouth and sucking gently.

A moan escaped her, and Lucas damn near lost all thought and threw caution to the wind at the sound of her pleasure. Pleasure, *he* was giving her.

Pleasure, he had no right to be giving her at this moment—or any other.

Lady Pippa had given him shelter…and he was all but betrothed to Lady Natalie, who awaited his arrival at the neighboring estate. Yet, Lucas, scoundrel that he was, held and kissed another. Imagined undressing this dark-haired beauty, instead of—Lucas had no idea what Lady Natalie looked like—and he found he could care less.

It was the woman in his arms that he wanted—in this moment, and all that followed.

He released her lobe, and she let out a disgruntled sigh, pushing her body ever closer to his as if she didn't realize the danger she was in—the threat he posed to her future.

A loud clap of thunder shook the front door on its hinges, and Pippa gasped, jumping back.

Her gaze darted around the room as if her brain hadn't registered the origin of the noise that had startled her.

"It was thunder," he called, balling his hands into fists to stop himself from reaching for her once more. "Only the storm."

She breathed heavily, not saying a word, and her hands clutched her chest—her bosom straining against the fabric of her gown, demanding to be set free.

Or maybe that was only Lucas's imagination begging him to step forward and take her in his arms again.

A deep crimson stain crept up her neck, and her face flamed red.

"My lord," she gushed. "I am...I am so sorry. I have acted most improper. Whatever must you think of me?"

On the tip of his tongue were the many words he wanted to say about her: sensual, erotic, alluring, beautiful, caring, compassionate, and captivating. Given a minute longer, allowing his mind to clear, he would likely string together another ten words that adequately described her.

"You must think me a wanton woman, my lord."

As long as she was only wanton for him, Lucas would call her exactly that if it pleased her.

Too late, he realized his mistake at remaining silent so long as her body trembled and she stumbled farther from him.

She truly believed he thought negatively of her—and what had just occurred between them.

Pippa grabbed her skirts in her hand and fled the room. Her embarrassment evident to Lucas now—how had he not recognized the emotion before?

But he knew the answer.

The Earl of Maddox, heir to the Marquis of Bowmont, had never sought out any woman of respectable standing—nor had he the occasion to ruin a proper lady.

Bloody hell, Merry Christmastide to him.

If he was not already certain of his tendency to tarnish every situation, it was evident now.

Chapter Nine

Pippa noticed the sliver of light escaping the edges of her draperies the moment her eyes fluttered opened. She'd hurriedly donned a morning gown with an apron and pockets before pulling the heavy fabric aside—scared she'd be disappointed to find the storm still lingering. She was pleasantly surprised to see her first instinct was true. A patchy blue sky greeted her with the grey storm clouds clinging at the horizon, not completely ready to move on from Somerset. The tops of the trees stood tall with no wind pushing them to and fro—and below, a thin layer of snow dotted the landscape.

At least for today, the storm had been pushed aside.

The roads should be passable very soon. That meant three things: her parents would be arriving shortly, she'd be free to deliver her gifts and baked goods to the village, and Lucas would be journeying on to Lady Natalie's Christmas party. Her excitement for the first two diminished with the thought of Lucas's departure—from her home and her life.

A Kiss At Christmastide

It was irrational to think a man, this complete stranger, would happen upon her house during a storm and become a permanent fixture in her life. Their paths had only crossed for these short two days—they would both move on from here, each forgetting the other. There was the possibility of them meeting again when Pippa returned to London. Would they nod to one another—possibly dance a set, or share refreshments at the opera—or would they both look the other way, agreeing to keep the memory of their time together intact without ruining the specialness by seeking to continue their acquaintance?

An acquaintance that would lead nowhere.

Regardless of what their futures held, today, they would go their separate ways. She to the village, and Lucas to his party—although, two days late, yet still in time for the holiday.

Pippa smiled, realizing that, although times would return to normal, she'd fulfilled what her parents had found…love during the Christmastide. That she'd kissed a man most unsuitable did not matter, did it? When in his arms, he did not feel the least bit as Pippa imagined a rogue would feel.

Their kiss had been everything she'd anticipated, and yet, far exceeded her expectations. His lips had been warm and intense. His hands had caressed her bum, kneading in gentlest of fashions. His scent had invaded her senses—he smelled of all things manly, pine and leather with a hint of sandalwood.

He'd been in control of their kiss; however, he hadn't sought to prove his dominance—nor take their intimate moment further than Pippa was prepared for. If Lucas would have asked, or led, she more than likely would have allowed him any liberties he sought.

It was a startling thought, and confirmed that he needed to go immediately; move on to Lady Natalie's party. If he stayed, it would not be him leading her to ruin, but Pippa walking into her own undoing—with no reservations.

Did every man's kiss affect women in such a way? Pippa did not expect so. There had been Mr. Gordon Everdom, who'd asked her to dance twice at one ball—but his hands were clammy and damp. His scent was that of a savory duck soup, as if his meal were exiting through his pores as the night progressed and his body became overheated. Pippa enjoyed duck soup as much as the next miss, but not as a perfume. It had never crossed Pippa's mind to allow his lips anywhere near hers. Not for fear of a scandal, but that she knew there would be no pleasure to be found in Everdom's arms.

All night, she'd longed for Lucas's lips to return to hers, continue the dance they'd started the night before, moving against one another to a beat only they heard.

Pippa's first kiss—and it had been far grander than she and Lady Natalie had dreamt of in their youths. They'd been so naïve to think their first kisses would come on their wedding days to the men who'd sweep them off their feet and make their girlish fairytale dreams come true.

Had Lady Natalie met her Prince Charming? Had he swept her off her feet?

Lucas was no Prince Charming. Even as little as she knew of him, she suspected he lived in the darkness far more than the light. Pippa could not see herself following any man into that existence, which suited her well because Lucas would be gone within the next few hours, and their kiss would remain an exquisite memory to be cherished and re-lived during the years to come—and best during the deep nighttime hours.

It did not matter if Natalie's beau was charming, wealthy, and from a good family, for Pippa would certainly secure a favorable match with time. Possibly before the next Christmastide season.

But could she leave fate to chance? The need to return to London and give herself the opportunity for another Season was a necessity.

For now, she had gifts to prepare, and a village full of tenants to see.

She rushed down the stairs, renewed at the thought of venturing out as she was no longer trapped by the storm. Though, oddly, she hadn't felt trapped and alone since Lucas's arrival. In fact, she seemed unable to escape him no matter where she hid in the house—not that Pippa would admit that she'd sought out the kitchen the night before to escape his notice, thinking a place where servants gathered was safe and beyond detection of a man such as Lucas.

There was much to do, so many things she'd neglected since his arrival. Neglect wasn't the correct word at all. There were things she'd outright forgotten since he'd stepped into her home and taken over her every thought—such as the children. The village children depended on gifts from her and her mother to stay warm during the winter months. New caps, capes, muffs, mittens, and socks. Many Londoners would be shocked to know that Pippa spent a great deal of time on her charitable pursuits, though she did not view the less fortunate as such. Nor did she speak to anyone of her caring heart. From her mother, Pippa had learned the misfortune of being born to a lower class—a life many saw as inescapable. Nonetheless, her mother,

Cordelia, had escaped her impoverished life but was one of the few that always looked back as opposed to forward. She had taught her daughter a life lesson that many young debutantes never learned.

Kindness.

The art of being genuinely caring to all.

One could never know a person's past or the wounds they'd suffered. Therefore, it was nobody's right to judge another.

However, it *was* her duty to help in any way she could.

It made Pippa's attitude toward Lady Natalie's betrayal and her spiteful meeting with Lucas all the more concerning. She'd wished ill will on another voluntarily— it was unwarrantable. Pippa would double her good deeds to redeem herself in her own eyes.

But first, she needed to prepare all the packages for delivery. Thankfully, Cook had arrived early to finish baking the pies Pippa had forgotten in the kitchen— sidetracked by Lucas's kiss.

Hurrying to her mother's parlor, Pippa began wrapping a book, cap, mittens or a muff, and cape in brown paper she'd had her father bring back from London a few months past. It would keep the gifts dry if it were snowing while she was out delivering them. Each was tied with a bow, green for the boys and red for the girls. It was Christmas, after all. No pink and blue.

Last year, she'd given school essentials: individual chalkboards, pencils, and school primers. And the year before that, she'd begged her father for a new pair of shoes for each child. It had been a grand year. Pippa had taught a few lessons to the children before preparing for her own entrance into society—where lowering oneself to a position of pay was deemed unfit and disreputable. She longed to return to that simpler time when she'd actively pursued what made her happy, not what looked best for a young woman of high breeding. She held no illusions that when she wed, her husband would not look proudly on a woman who sought happiness among the less fortunate.

Men such as the Duke of Midcrest, her father, rarely existed in society.

Before long, Pippa moved from her hunched position near the low table in favor of sitting prone on the rug near the crackling hearth. The warmth was welcome without being overpowering. She'd spent several hours the day before bringing merriment to this room, her mother's chosen space, and it increased her spirit greatly knowing her dear mother would soon join her. Though the holiday hadn't started with promise, she was certain all would be put to rights by the end of the day.

Lucas would be gone—as regrettable as that was to her—and her parents would arrive. Her mother would take to the kitchen, with Pippa's help, and they would prepare their family feast, while her father wrapped gifts for his two beloved women. It was the normal way of things.

With the confusion Lucas's arrival and their kiss had brought, Pippa desperately needed things to be normal. A few short hours to think through all the emotions coursing through her. They were foreign, yet not completely unwanted, and something she needed to explore, especially if she were serious about taking a husband.

When she did settle on the perfect man, he would be tall, his arms strong, and his gaze intense—his hair falling just over his eyes in that rakish sort of way she hadn't given much thought to in previous days. A humorous spirit would be much preferred, and she certainly enjoyed good-natured bantering.

The image that sprang to mind had Pippa's eyes opening wide in shock—why did her future husband so accurately resemble Lucas. Certainly, her mind was playing tricks on her, for a man like Lucas was the exact type of man she should run far away from.

Pippa tied the last ribbon on the final gift and pushed to her feet to take in all she'd accomplished. Twenty-seven tiny bundled packages with perfectly tied bows.

Her back ached, and her fingers were numb from trying so much ribbon.

She couldn't help but smile, though, thinking about the joy on the children's faces when she arrived at their doors bearing gifts.

A gong sounded from her father's study, and Pippa paused to count—eleven. If she planned to have sufficient time to load her carriage, deliver all the gifts, and return before her parents' arrival, Pippa needed to hurry.

"Lady Pippa?" Briars called, stepping into the room.

"Yes?" Pippa turned to face her family's aging servant, who seemed unable to hide his smile at the many presents wrapped and waiting for tiny hands to open them. One such gift had been specially wrapped for Briars' own granddaughter; a precocious six-year-old with raven hair and the greenest of eyes—ever so intense for one so young.

"The carriage is readied and being brought round for you." Briars was a dear soul and looked after Pippa during the rare times her parents were away. His children and grandchildren were very lucky to have such a man of standing as their patriarch. "Please, let me know if you require anything further."

"The roads have dried enough for travel?" There was little reason to load the carriage and set out only to get stuck or be forced to turn back due to impassible conditions. She'd be lying if a part of her longed to have the butler tell her things were still negatively impacted by the passing storm. The children would not get their gifts, but she'd have more time with Lucas—maybe even another kiss.

"Yes, my lady."

"That is wonderful news." Pippa smiled brightly, her joy going no further than her lips. "I will bring everything to the foyer to be loaded."

"I will have a footman sent to assist you."

"That is not necessary," Pippa assured him. "They are light, but do have him bring the pies from the kitchen."

"Certainly." With a quick nod, he was on his way, leaving the door open for her to move the presents.

Pippa could hear two maids giggling through the open door over a gift one of the girls had received from a particularly unsuitable suitor. In that instant, she missed her dear friend, Natalie. They would have gossiped for hours if one of them had received a Christmas gift—from a man. After her kiss the night before, Pippa would have braved the storm to journey all the way to the neighboring estate just to gush over how handsome Lucas was. But that was not how things were to be. What hurt most was not knowing the reason she'd lost her friend. Had it been something Pippa had done or said? Was it that Natalie had found their friendship had outlasted its usefulness? She did not believe that to be true in any way.

But there was nothing she could do about Lady Natalie and her decision to end their friendship in such a cruel manner.

It was hard to push from her mind the thought of her dear friend entering into a betrothal, and all before Pippa knew anything of the man. Was he worthy of Natalie's love? Did he love her in return? Where was his estate? Would Natalie be allowed time to visit with her friends?

Pippa sighed, collecting as many presents as she could and hurried to the foyer, depositing the pile as she turned to gather more.

"Good day, Lady Pippa."

She froze at the deep tone, the words drawled slow enough to linger far longer than was necessary for the "Ps" in her name. His voice was sweeter than a summer batch of honey collected not far from her manor house. However, nothing in his tone confirmed that he was ever willingly labeled as "sweet." He was more of a blackberry, dark and forbidding on the outside, but sugary and delicious on the inside. One only need journey past his menacing exterior.

Delicious? It was an odd term to use to define a man. Or any person for that matter.

Though it fit Lucas—and her feelings toward him—perfectly.

"Good morn, my lord." Pippa's voice wobbled slightly. "I do hope your rest was revitalizing."

"I have discovered many revitalizing things since my arrival in Somerset."

Pippa blinked rapidly and swallowed past the sawdust that dried her throat at his inciting words. She would not read too much into his comment, she would not read too much into his comment—she would *not* read too much into his comment.

"You look dashing today and ready to venture forth to your holiday party," she said, refusing to address his earlier words. "I have noticed the storm has moved to the horizon, and Briars informed me the roads are now passable."

He released a sigh, and Pippa could have sworn he muttered the word "pity."

Again, she would not bite.

"What are you doing?" He took the final two steps into the entry and surveyed her pile of gifts. "It looks as if you have been busy since we parted last night."

Another reference to the previous night—and their kiss. "I am preparing to depart for the village to deliver gifts." Her words were safe enough, and they left her mouth without a hitch, even though she felt her skin warming the closer he came to her. "There is nothing stopping me now, and I have much to attend to."

"Ah, yes," he said. He picked up a package wrapped with a green bow. "For the children. A bleeding heart."

He'd retreated to the demeanor from his arrival— cold and removed.

No longer was he the man who'd helped her in the kitchens or given her the gift of a kiss.

"A bleeding heart?" she asked.

"Certainly," he confirmed what she'd thought she'd heard him say. "You will put your safety in jeopardy for others. The storm has moved inland, but that does not mean it will stay there for long."

She knew he spoke the truth of the matter for it was common for storms to pass with another close behind. "For now, the weather is clear enough, my lord."

"Lucas."

By morning light, Pippa did not feel comfortable addressing him by his given name. It was a shame, but she felt the connection they'd shared the day before was gone. He was an earl, a wealthy man, and needed to continue on to Lady Natalie's. It was where he belonged. While Pippa, she belonged here or in the village.

"Anyways, Lucas," Pippa continued, unfazed—or at least unwilling to show him how he affected her. "I will bid you farewell. You will likely arrive at your destination long before I return from the village."

"More's the pity." There it was again, his words begging her to comment. "Do you need assistance?" He looked around as if expecting a footman to appear.

"The carriage is being brought round, but thank you."

He placed the gift he'd picked up back on the stack and turned his intense stare to her. "I have had a fascinating two days, Lady Pippa. I thank you for not banishing me to the stables for shelter."

Pippa chuckled, knowing she'd been tempted by his dour mood that first night to do just that. "And I thank you for helping in the kitchen last night." She purposefully didn't mention what had happened after their time in the kitchen.

"It was an experience completely new to me."

"Not completely new, may I remind you." Pippa was happy he was willing to let slide their kiss. "You were quite accomplished with the pie crusts."

"Ah, yes, very true," he said, tapping his finger against his chin. "It had slipped my mind...as there were more memorable moments."

She'd counted her blessings too soon it would seem. Of course, she would not want to forget their kiss. But surely, Lucas had kissed many, many, many women and would not allow their kiss to take up so much space in his thoughts. But maybe, just maybe, he was similarly affected by their intimate moment.

The front door opened to reveal her waiting carriage—Lucas's horse saddled nearby.

"You will continue on horseback?" she asked, a bit downcast knowing he'd already made plans to depart.

He looked out the open door as the footman collected Pippa's gifts to load in her carriage. "Yes, I fear my carriage is suitably stuck in the muck on the main road. But as you've said, the storm has moved to the horizon and the time has come for me to be on my way. Your hospitality, though lacking at first, was remedied and greatly appreciated, my lady."

"I do appreciate you overlooking my abysmal manners." Pippa wanted to thank him, but could not find the adequate words to express exactly what she was thankful for—his presence while she'd been alone, his help in the kitchen, or his part in showing her that passion existed for her. "Please, give Lady Natalie and her family my kindest regards."

He gazed once more out the open door and then back to her, his eyes taking her in from head to toe. "It is likely to be very cold outside, and the temperatures are dropping rapidly, please wear sufficient protection against the elements."

It was a glimpse of the Lucas she'd met the previous night, and she adored that side of him. It was something he was very uncomfortable with showing people, as was evident from his stance and knitted brow.

"I certainly will." At his dubious look, she continued, "There are many warm blankets in my carriage, and my coat with fur is just over there." Pippa nodded to her coat, hanging close to the door.

"Can I not talk you into accompanying me to the Sheridans?"

"I am afraid not, my lord." She'd escaped telling him the details of her falling-out with Natalie, and she wanted to keep it that way. If Natalie chose to tell others, that was her right. But never would Pippa speak ill of a friend, no matter how hurt and abandoned she felt. "I will await my parents' arrival."

It was an excuse—and he saw right through it, but thankfully, he did not press her.

Even her parents likely expected her to journey to Lady Natalie's party and would not be concerned if they arrived to a note to that effect.

Still, they lingered...

Pippa was not ready to walk out the door and possibly never see him again.

Yet, she was unsure of his reason for remaining. The roads were clear, and a new distraction awaited him only a mile down the road.

She'd met men like him before, always departing for another adventure before the one before had concluded. The allure of something new and exciting was something Pippa could understand, just not something she always *needed* for herself.

People got hurt when one lived that way—thankfully, she had no attachment to Lucas. He could leave, and she would go on as she always had.

If that were true, why was an empty hole forming in her middle? A sinking feeling that things would not, in fact, return to normal after his departure, but rather that a void would be left...emptiness not easily filled.

"It has been enjoyable, my lord."

"For me as well, my lady." With a small bow, Lucas turned a rakish grin in her direction, sending her heart fluttering. "Farewell, until we meet again."

And, as unexpectedly as he'd arrived in her life, Lucas, the Earl of Maddox, disappeared.

A Kiss At Christmastide

He sauntered out the door without so much as a glance over his shoulder. However, he only made it a few feet before freezing in his tracks, his shoulders straightening as tension took over his entire body.

Chapter Ten

Every inch of Lucas's body was on high alert, taut and expectant, as he stared at the group who stood in Pippa's drive. His parents, the Marquis and Marchioness of Bowmont were flanked by the Duke and Duchess of Sheridan, a young blonde woman at their side. Behind them, another carriage, the trunk loaded high with traveling luggage, stopped, and an elder couple disembarked to join the growing party.

Lucas hadn't arrived in a timely manner, so it appeared the party had gone in search of him—how would they know to find him here?

"Good day, Father." Lucas nodded in his father's direction as the man brought his monocle to his eye to assure him that it was, indeed, his wayward rakehell of a son. "And to you, Mother." He bowed to his mother, who stared down her nose at her remaining son, disappointment written on her face. It was the exact look he'd run from all these years—and it had the same effect on him now as it had when he was just a boy who'd lost his younger brother, his best friend.

The stately pair had aged since he'd seen them last, the edges of his father's neatly trimmed hair had greyed, and his mother did not stand nearly as tall as he remembered. Had it been the loss of not only one son, but two, that made the couple appear a decade older than they should? However, they were still the aloof and unaffected couple they'd been following Randolph's passing. Lucas was not worthy to be in their presence, and their expressions conveyed their distaste to all who were watching.

"Maddox," his father said gruffly. "We worried you'd come to harm—possibly been set upon by highwaymen."

"I'm sorry for your misfortune, Father," Lucas retorted, careful to keep his tone even and distant—after his father called him by his title, not his given name. "My carriage became stranded on the main road, and I sought shelter at Helton House until I could continue on."

"You were scheduled to arrive at the holiday party a full day before the storm hit."

"Yes, well, I found I had pressing matters to attend to, which delayed my departure from London by a day." He didn't owe them any explanation, though he felt compelled to give one with all the eyes on him.

"Lucas," Pippa called. He glanced over his shoulder, willing her to shut the door and forget about him before anyone set eyes on her. It was not to be. She walked out the open door and stood beside him, her smile infectious. "Mother, Father, you have arrived. I was so worried!"

She was down the front steps and before her parents within an instant as they hugged and more greetings were shared.

Not far from the trio, his parents, the duke, and duchess, and Lady Natalie—it could be no other—stood, stock-still, watching the overly affectionate family with disgust. Even his father's lip curled slightly at the open display of love before them.

"Lady Pippa is found in another compromising situation—alone with a gentleman for what...two full days?" the blonde woman whispered loud enough for all to hear. "Even after fleeing London, scandal finds her in the country."

"I am more concerned with the man," the Duke of Sheridan said. "Carrying on thusly—very bad for my family name, my daughter, and my business."

"This does complicate things greatly," the marchioness confirmed. "Delward, what do you propose is to happen?"

"There is nothing compromising or concerning about any of this," Lucas stated loudly, yet no one present acknowledged that he was even there for this exchange of words that greatly affected his current situation—and his future.

Lucas's father dropped his eyepiece and shook his head. The strikes against Lucas continued to mount.

"They are still properly betrothed," Lucas's father chimed in. "The paperwork is drafted and signed by all who matter. The banns are to be read in a few weeks' time. I suppose our agreed upon dowry settlement could be adjusted to compensate for our son's lack of decorum."

"I am not—" he started to deny again.

"Betrothed?" Pippa asked. Her faced drained of all color as she looked between Lucas, his father, and Lady Natalie—the girl's smirk irritating Lucas greatly. "Is that true?"

Lucas shook his head, his posture longing to deny the accusation, yet he would not verbally lie to Pippa. He'd known the reasoning behind his invitation to Lady Natalie's country estate. His parents had found a suitable match for their scoundrel of a son—and, misguidedly, Lucas had contemplated the notion of reconciliation between him and his parents. He would never admit that aloud either, but there it was, true to his core.

They did not want to know their surviving son. They had no intention of allowing him to be a part of their lives. No matter how earnestly Lucas had wanted that outcome.

No, they were calling in their dues. Lucas was responsible for the death of his young brother, and his parents meant to have their retribution for that tragedy. But no amount of repentance would raise his level in their estimation.

In a few years, they would demand something more of him, and more, and more, until Lucas did not recognize his life.

"Pippa, I—"

"You owe me no explanation," she choked out, failing to hide her pain over his deception. "I am only sad you did not feel you could be truthful with me."

"If I could go back…" Lucas let his words trail off, unsure how to complete his thought.

Up until the previous night, he'd been more than willing to give in to his parents' demands—marry a girl he'd never met, gain his father yet another business ally, and continue on as he always had, his new wife set up in a procured townhouse and forgotten until the time came he inherited his father's vast estate and the married pair moved into the Bowmont townhouse.

"There is no need for all of that," Pippa slashed her hand through the air, signaling it was time for him to stay silent—allowing her to depart with her pride intact.

Everyone present stared at him. Pippa with tears in her eyes. Her parents showed concern for their daughter's well-being, and the rest held their breaths for him to deny ruining Lady Pippa.

For a brief moment, Lucas thought to confirm their suspicions and detangle himself from any attachment to Lady Natalie—but that would mean tarnishing Pippa's future, and likely, call for her father to demand Lucas wed Pippa immediately.

He could not do such a thing to Pippa—he'd come to care for her, and saddling her with a rakehell for a husband was not a fate he'd ever wish upon her, even though he longed to make her his.

"Lady Pippa—" Lucas needed to do the right thing…to be noble and ignore what the people might think of him because his concern for her and her future far outweighed others' opinions of him. He'd never sought to ruin her, even if he could never have her for himself. "I'm here despite Pippa's best efforts to get rid of me, though the storm did not allow it. She was forced to house my servants and me, and that should not result in any wrong impressions being attached to her person."

His words once again fell on deaf ears. Not a single person registered his defense of Lady Pippa, he wondered if they even noticed him slip and address her by her given name. He was a rake, a scoundrel, but never should his reputation result in her ruination.

"Let us go inside. I wish you all a merry Christmastide celebration." Pippa lifted her gaze, keeping her head high as she took hold of her mother's arm and started toward

Lucas. He hoped she'd stop, say something to him, invite him to meet her parents. However, the trio walked right past him without acknowledging his presence.

The door shut soundly behind them with a solid thud.

"Come, boy," his father called, motioning Lucas to his side. "We have much to discuss and settle upon before anyone can enjoy the coming announcement."

Nothing about Christmastide. Not a word of spending their first holiday together in many years. Lucas almost felt ridiculous for the tiny gift he'd purchased for his mother before leaving London—a heart-shaped brooch.

It had been a silly, impulsive purchase by a man who remembered the boy who'd adored his parents.

Lucas hadn't demanded their respect, nor asked for their love then—and he certainly did not want it now.

Glancing over his shoulder, Lucas looked to the tightly closed door to Helton House.

Pippa was upset and hurt. She had every right to feel that way. He'd been misleading her since his arrival and had never thought she'd find out about his parents' plans for him, or figure he'd care if she did.

But he cared. An emotion he'd felt long dead with Randolph.

...his own bleeding heart surfaced.

As his mother was more than willing to admit, Lucas did not deserve anything worth having in life. His misdeeds were too debilitating.

Pippa would surely find happiness and a future if Lucas were not a part of her life. He knew he'd be required to marry Lady Natalie to make certain word did not spread of their association, as innocent as it had been. Which was extremely innocent compared to Lucas's past transgressions.

With Lady Natalie as his wife, her family would all be required to keep this scandal from spreading. No parent wants to see their daughter's betrothed connected to the ruination of a young woman.

His father had been correct in this one thing: it would be bad for business and all of their family names.

Lucas didn't care about his father's business or his family name. He only cared that Pippa stayed above reproach and away from any hint of scandal.

The time had finally come for Lucas to sacrifice himself, pay his dues for all that'd happened in his past—there were far worse things than being tied to a woman you did not love.

Giving up a woman you *could* love was certainly one of those things.

Chapter Eleven

Pippa stood with her back against the front door and listened as the carriage pulled away. The horses' hooves clopped against the cobblestoned drive as they departed. For the first time, she longed for the storm to continue raging outside to obscure the sound. Her eyes remained closed, though she felt her mother's stare. She could not face either of her parents. They'd worked entirely too hard to overcome their own scandalous past for Pippa to bring gossip down on them once again.

She'd done an inconceivable, horrendous thing. She'd been lost in the moment, and had allowed her good breeding to slip and her desires to take hold of her. Neither Cordelia nor her father, Gerald, were worried about any type of scandal. No, they were worried only about Pippa—they'd likely been interested to meet Lucas, witnessing the unspoken bond between their daughter and the Earl of Maddox.

That had been made impossible after Pippa had slammed the door—not directly in his face, but to his back as he'd kept his eyes trained on Lady Natalie. Was it conceivable that she felt as secure in Lucas's arms as Pippa had? Maybe both women were being taken advantage of by that rakehell.

Pippa hadn't any answers, and would likely never receive them.

Lucas had left with his parents and the Sheridans in their carriage. He'd go on to enjoy the holiday at Natalie's estate, and with luck—and a lowering of the agreed dowry—would be officially betrothed to Pippa's former friend by the New Year.

And Pippa would be alone in Somerset.

Yet, it was a certainty she'd run across the pair if they were to wed. Lucas and Natalie would spend holidays and such with Natalie's family in Somerset.

The agony of the future to come was only overshadowed by the senseless heartbreak Pippa felt.

Lucas had allowed Pippa to walk past and hadn't so much as tried to stop her to explain—that only meant there was no reasonable explanation. Lucas had come into her home, knowing he was betrothed to Lady Natalie and had set out to deceive Pippa.

It hurt.

It wounded far worse than anything Natalie had done to end their long-standing friendship.

Lucas had preyed on Pippa's weaknesses and had brought about her irrevocable ruin. She'd thought he was held down by some burden too extreme, far too dark to allow her in. Somewhere deep inside, Pippa had thought she was helping Lucas, giving him a few short days of merriment after so many years separated from family during a season of great joy.

That hadn't been the case.

Pippa's hurt turned to anger, and she pushed away from the door, stalking toward the main staircase.

"Pippy?" her mother called, using her childhood name. "Please, speak to your father and me. We are ever so worried—and more than a bit confused over what transpired outside."

She paused on the first landing and looked back toward her parents. They did not deserve her harsh treatment and cruel words. "Nothing untoward happened, I can assure you both of that. Not that it means much." Pippa threw the words over her shoulder before starting up the stairs, once more.

Lucas had been all but betrothed the entire time. All the mentions of Lady Natalie, Pippa and Natalie's friendship, and the holiday party—not once had he shared who he truly was. They were likely already discussing all Pippa had shared about the end of her and Natalie's friendship. Her former friend probably found joy in the telling of how Lucas and Pippa had been utterly embarrassed in front of a teeming room. The saddest part was that Pippa knew the sound of his snide chuckle—the sound he made when he heard something witty that poked fun at another. She hadn't heard it since his first moments in her home, but Pippa would never forget the sound.

Mainly because there was a lonesome sadness to it that hinted, once again, at a wound—almost as if he weren't making light of the jest spoken but needing an outlet for his pent-up hurt and anger.

At first, Pippa had mistaken his conduct for a cross-personality, but she no longer felt that was at the core of his drastic shifts in character.

"Pippy!" her father shouted as she stomped up the stairs. "Do come back here this instant and explain this entire mess."

Pippa didn't stop. She didn't look over her shoulder or answer his calls. Without saying the words, her father was blaming her for the scene outside, the uncomfortable debacle between her family and Natalie's. But it wasn't her fault. The culpability most definitely lay at Lucas's feet, not hers.

Her anger was swiftly intensifying to fury—and she would prefer her parents not witness her breakdown, for she knew that was to come. How could it not follow?

And it was all for a man she hadn't wanted in her home to begin with. She should have sent him to the stables for shelter until the storm passed. It was more than he deserved.

Pippa had half a mind to wish she'd have made him return to his carriage and refused him altogether; yet, that would be wishing certain ill will on another.

That scoundrel of a man should be thankful she was not a spiteful woman.

She wanted to throw something, slam the wall—scream in a fit of rage, but instead, her shoulders shook with her weakness…her bleeding heart, as he'd called it.

What right did she have to be infuriated in the first place?

Lucas had made no promises to her. They had shared only a kiss, nothing more. Unless you counted his hands on her and his firmness pressed to her most tender spot. Could actions be taken as a promise—an agreement of something further?

They'd never spoken of anything past last night. He'd made no mention of a future, and neither did she know anything about his past.

The truth was that he hadn't thought enough of Pippa to share his connection with Lady Natalie.

Pippa was being irrational. Her expectations and feelings were misguided, at best. The idea that a genuine affection had developed between them in such a short time was childish. Warm fondness was based on open knowledge between two people. Sharing. In no way had she and Lucas had any sort of open communication or understanding.

Her lips tingled at the thought of his mouth on hers—his hands circling her waist to hold her tight. She shook her head, dispelling the thought. There were no feelings on his side, he was betrothed to another. A man promised to wed does not so easily hold another woman, should not crave her lips nor press his body against hers in need.

In fact, he'd outright deceived her.

Openly, willingly, and with full knowledge, he had duped her.

And stolen her first kiss.

The blackguard. The scoundrel. The debaucher of women.

He was a true London rakehell.

And Pippa hadn't seen past his motives to see his true nature. Lady Natalie and Lucas deserved each other—both selfish, vain creatures who sought their own happiness at the expense of others.

She stood on the top landing, breathing shallow, quick breaths.

At some point, her father had stopped shouting for her from below. However, Pippa was unaware when or how long she'd stood there.

Her legs ached from climbing the stairs quickly, so she must not have stood there overly long. Neither had a servant happened upon her. Though, the likelihood she would have noticed a servant through her anger was doubtful.

And Pippa would admit she was spitting mad, at herself for not seeing through his guise of the gentleman in need of shelter. He had duped her, and she hadn't had enough sense to see it happening.

Not even Lady Natalie's misplaced announcement all those months ago had Pippa spinning in such a way.

Possibly because Pippa knew she had no right to be cross with Lucas, to feel betrayed. He'd sought shelter during a storm, not asked to seduce her. Even their kiss could be blamed on her clumsy nature—though she hadn't any previous record of such ungainliness.

Every part of her wanted to be mad at him. Every inch of her wanted to march after the Sheridan carriage and speak her mind. Every logical instinct told her that Lucas wasn't entirely to blame for any of this. It was her unreal expectations of their kiss.

All that her parents had promised in a first kiss.

Their kiss that had ended with their undeniable love.

Pippa had desired a kiss, no matter how little she knew of the Earl of Maddox.

He'd given her a false impression, an expectation of more when he should have known not to offer Pippa any such thing.

The urge to stomp her foot and scream at her credulous character was almost too much to hold at bay.

"My lady."

She hadn't heard her trusted family servant traverse the stairs to her. She was not surprised her parents had sent him in their stead. Pippa patted her face, searching for any treacherous tears, which may have escaped her notice, before pasting a feeble smile on her face and turning.

Pippa was unsure what she'd expected to see in Briars' stare, but what greeted her almost had tears falling once more. His shoulders drooped, and his spine caved inward far more than normal—so much so, that he gazed at Pippa from a lower stature, though at one time, he'd stood far above her average height.

"Will you be needing the carriage, or shall I send the horses back to the stables?" he asked with regret. Her servants had been watching her, possibly hiding just out of sight, but close enough to hear all that had transpired between Pippa and Lucas.

Disappointment flared. She'd thought only of herself—and had forgotten the children. Again.

Pippa released her grip on the stair rail, her fingers aching at the action as she hadn't realized she'd been holding it so tightly. It was the only thing keeping her upright as her knees shook with weakness. Responsibility pulled the hurt from her and restored her sense of priority.

Certainly, Lucas hadn't seen her as a priority after he'd walked through her front door—no, he'd chosen Natalie, apparent by their departure together. It was time Pippa put first those who'd stood by her during her first Season, who hadn't joined the gossip rags in sensationalizing any affection or attraction Pippa had toward her music tutor.

The village. *Her* village. Though the small community sat nestled between Lady Natalie's estate and her own, they were hers. Many of them were related through blood kinship to her mother, and the rest gained at least part of their family income from the Midcrest dukedom.

Lady Natalie had been given the classic fair beauty most men favored. She was the daughter of a man far more influential than Pippa's. She'd had everything a girl could want since birth. When would Pippa receive what she desired? It was unfair the way Natalie treated Pippa, but her actions had gone unpunished, and still, she flourished.

"I will travel to the village as soon as I collect an extra muff," Pippa said, fearing Briars suspected she'd forgotten her duties for the day. "It is still blustery outside, and I have many gifts to deliver. I would not want to catch a cold before our Christmastide feast."

"Surely you are correct, Lady Pippa." He nodded at her forethought. "I will have the coachman await you in the drive and instruct the footman to load your gifts and the pies."

"Very good. I will only be a moment."

Pippa couldn't meet his stare, worried pity would be glaring back at her. It was something she could not handle, knowing that others—besides her—had witnessed the connection between Lucas and her. Everyone but Lucas, that is. Had he had such special moments with so many women that he didn't notice the rarity of it with her?

Hurrying to her room, Pippa searched for her extra muff.

She needed to focus on her future, not the past or Lucas. He was never meant to be hers, nor were they ever destined to meet. Their kiss was something that should have never happened. The draw of her parents' great love match was to blame—that was all. Nothing more. Nothing less.

She closed her eyes once more, and the feel of his lips against hers still seared her mouth—she could imagine them pressed together as if he were there.

Pressing her fingers to her lips, Pippa's pulse raced as she allowed herself this final moment to remember their kiss—a kiss that had affected them both in that split second of time.

Pippa let her hand fall limply to her side and, with it, she banished the feel of Lucas's arms around her. She pushed the scent of him from her senses, and she begged her mind to forget the set of his jaw and the wave in his hair.

It was done. He was gone.

And she had a life to live.

She spotted her warm, grey muff on her dressing table. Retrieving it, she made her way downstairs—a new set to her brow and determination in her step.

With a stop in the kitchen to make sure all was loaded and not a pie forgotten, Pippa would be on her way.

And after that, she did not know. She only knew what the next several hours held for her.

The kitchen was much as it had been the night before: supplies, flour, and sugar everywhere. A large pot boiled on the stove, and bread could be smelled baking in the oven as a tray of berry tarts cooled by the open window.

Her mother stood, kneading dough. The sight had tears springing to Pippa's eyes—it was as things should have been all along. Her mother, father, and her together for the holiday. They would laugh, bake desserts, prepare their feast, and spend the special day together before returning to London after the New Year began.

Then why did Pippa only feel regret, a sense of emptiness filling her more and more?

She was surrounded by the loved ones she'd prayed would arrive before Christmastide, but suddenly, they weren't enough—something, no, some*one* was missing.

And she needed to face the fact that he was never coming back. Never again would they work side by side in this very kitchen. Never again would they deck the halls of Helton House with festive cheer. Never again would he be there to brush a tear from her cheek when something saddened her.

"My dear Pippy," her mother called, keeping her eyes on the dough she kneaded and her back to her daughter.

"Yes, Mother, I am here."

"I knew you were," she continued. "You bring a heart far heavier than this season calls for."

"My disposition will improve before the holiday comes, Mother, I promise," Pippa said, wishing she'd departed instead of making one final trip to the kitchen. She did not seek to cast a dark shadow on everyone. "When I return from the village, my spirits will be joyous and cheerful once again."

With a smile, Cordelia turned to face her daughter, and Pippa's chest ached at the pain she'd caused her mother.

"May I offer a few words of advice?" Cordelia wiped her hands on her apron as she walked towards Pippa. "It is something my mother told me many years ago, but during any time I doubt my decisions, I repeat the words aloud."

Pippa nodded as her lip trembled. It would only serve to make her mother feel worse if Pippa let the sob she held back pass her lips.

"Very well. And know you may not find meaning in my words now, but one day...one day, you will." Her mother gathered Pippa in her arms and hugged her tightly, whispering the next words in her ear—as if it were a long-kept secret they could not risk others overhearing as the magic within them would fade. "Life—and love—are much like a storm. The storm that kept your father and me away, in fact, and even now threatens to return. The clouds, the wind, the rain may make it impossible for you to see a clear path to your fated destination, but with time and a lot of faith, you will find the correct path once more—or a better path, one that could not be seen before the storm made it visible. But remember, another storm may try to dissuade you, but keep going, keep moving, and when the storm passes, so will your doubts and concerns be pushed away with the clouds, revealing your next course."

Her mother was correct as only hints of the meaning behind her mother's advice stuck with Pippa. The storm had brought Lucas to her—and with its departure, it had taken him from her. If that was where her path led, away from Lucas, then so be it. But that did not make her long any less to be on the same path as he.

"Promise me something, my dear girl," Cordelia said before pulling back, holding Pippa at arm's length.

"Anything, Mother," Pippa agreed, knowing she'd likely not be able to keep the promise she was about to make.

"Have faith, open your heart and, most of all, listen to what others have to say."

It all sounded so very simple. "Yes, I will always hold tight to my faith and listen to others."

"And your heart—it will remain open?" her mother asked.

"I will do my very best," Pippa said.

"Very good." She placed a kiss to each of Pippa's cheeks. "Now, hurry along. Do give my best wishes to all in the village. I have much work to do before tomorrow."

Pippa fled the kitchen as her mother returned to knead the dough.

Chapter Twelve

"As you can see, my family and our lineage are not in question," Sheridan said as he led Lucas and his father into the study. "I understand the importance of marrying my daughter to the future Marquis of Bowmont, but this..."—he paused to pour three tumblers of scotch—"...this new development calls for a renegotiation of our contract, Bowmont."

Lucas's father stood a foot inside the study door, refusing to accept the proffered spirits. Lucas had no qualms about accepting the drink, and threw it back in one gulp, holding the glass out to the duke for a refill.

Sheridan raised a brow at Lucas's forward nature, but took the tumbler and poured a healthy portion before turning back to the pair.

"I do not think the dowry needs adjustment," his father countered.

"Sit, Bowmont," the duke said, taking his own seat behind his massive desk. It was a move to show dominance and to remind Lucas's father that they were on Sheridan ground, not Bowmont—which meant his father needed to give up the upper hand. Reluctantly, his father moved farther into the room and set his hand on the high, winged-back chair, making no further move to sit. If he wasn't going to take the seat, Lucas was. He settled heavily into the chair with a loud creak. Sheridan cleared his throat before continuing. "Very well, stand, we can talk either way. I am leery of this match, if I'm honest."

Beyond his decision to stand, the marquis seemed unfazed by Sheridan's declaration. "My son is a man, and is therefore afforded certain liberties and freedoms. We had not presented the contract to Lucas yet—there are no grounds for redrafting the marriage settlement."

It was in Lucas's best interest to remain silent while his father and Sheridan openly discussed his future. If Lucas disputed the match, Pippa's name would be ruined. However, on the other hand, if these men came to an agreement, then he'd be tied to a woman he didn't know and would never love. What other choice did he have to save Pippa? She didn't deserve her name being tarnished or her family being ostracized within society. And he wouldn't jeopardize any match she could later make.

Lucas wanted Pippa for his own—yet, he could never be worthy of a woman such as she: loving, compassionate, and giving. Bloody hell, she spent her free time knitting caps for the less fortunate.

"My daughter has been injured—and if this betrothal is to go forward, she will be compensated for the injury your son has caused," Sheridan declared.

"My charity only runs so deep." Lucas didn't have to imagine the indignation in his father's words. The degradation of feelings was not something his father would ever admit as a genuine injury.

The only act of charity Lucas could claim was housing a mistress who'd been tossed from her bordello after her relationship with Lucas became public.

That had been many years ago. A lifetime ago, when he'd still thought to do anything to gain his parents' attention; good or bad. Though the Marquis and Marchioness of Bowmont had ignored his insolence and refused to address the scandal of their son coexisting with a woman of loose morals. He'd even dared to bring the woman to a society ball.

When it hadn't worked—and the woman expected marriage—Lucas had to break ties.

She deserved more, though he did not confuse this with an act of goodness. No, he'd allowed his mistress to seek other entanglements to save himself.

Aiding one's mistress was in no way comparable to helping a village full of children. Lucas was not foolish enough to think he was, in any way, worthy of Lady Pippa.

His best decision was to make this all disappear. Thankfully, that was something he had experience in. People around him disappeared—his little brother, his parents, his university friends, and a mistress or two.

And with them, their problems.

Though, Randolph's disappearance directly started Lucas's family breakdown; but his friends and his mistresses, when he pushed, they fled. Ultimately, they were better off without him.

Pippa would be best without him and the problems his presence would cause in her life. The only fail-safe plan was to wed Lady Natalie—and make sure no one ever spoke of his unchaperoned time with Lady Pippa. He'd known that demanding shelter was highly inappropriate, but he'd been wet, cold, and had a deuced headache from a night of drinking. And when he'd seen Pippa, well, Lucas wanted nothing more than to stay in her company as all sorts of sordid thoughts invaded his mind.

He was everything his parents claimed him to be.

Never to his face, of course, but behind closed doors, in whispers.

The Marquis and Marchioness of Bowmont would not admit it, but they were afraid of their son. Part of him wondered if they believed Lucas had led Randolph out to that slew, that none of it had been an accident, that Lucas hadn't lived with the pain and agony every moment of every day since.

How would they know anything—they'd never asked?

Never once had they asked if Lucas had known his brother followed him that night.

Not once had they asked if Lucas wished harm upon his younger sibling.

Never had they inquired whether Lucas wanted to go away and never return to his family home.

No, this was all discussed in hushed tones behind his parents' locked bedchamber door with Lucas brokenhearted and alone in the hall. The servants ignored him as if they'd all been instructed that both of the Bowmont boys had perished that fateful night by the creek—and no heir remained.

It was much like today, but Sheridan and his father did not speak in whispers nor did they hide behind a locked door.

"Now we speak of my daughter as if you are taking pity on her—doing me a gentlemanly favor, no less," Sheridan spit out, "...by taking her off my hands and wedding her to your degenerate of a son?"

"No matter my son's many shortcomings, he is my heir, and will one day be a marquis—and with that, will come everything I have amassed."

"*We* have amassed," the duke reminded Lucas's father. "I will not have you forget my instrumental part in your family's good fortune since our partnership began."

"I would dream of no such thing," Bowmont retorted. "In fact, I am doing the complete opposite by working toward marrying our families and solidifying our continued success."

His father seemed to know that Lucas would not fight any decision the two men settled on.

Not once, since the night of his brother's death, had Lucas forced his father—or his mother—to answer any of the questions he had, and neither had they addressed theirs. They were content with living separate lives, never asking, but also never hearing Lucas's side of all that had happened.

How Lucas had grieved for Randolph, the many times he'd thought relief would only be found once he joined his brother in the hereafter.

Peace—it was something Lucas had never experienced since that day.

To dream…

Lucas never dreamed, never thought or longed for what could be. He'd learned at a young age that it only led to tragedy and loneliness.

Except, that wasn't entirely true.

He'd forgotten himself, his past, his burdens, and his sorrows during those brief hours with Pippa. She'd banished his demons.

They'd tried to drag him back down during his walk about her estate—but he'd escaped them with her help and her Christmastide spirit. She'd refused to let him sink, though the weights dragging him down were invisible to her. Unbeknownst to Pippa, she'd untied the great burden that kept him below and allowed him to finally surface, something he couldn't remember doing since the night of his last adventure.

He'd taken his first breath in almost fifteen years.

Her light expelled his darkness, an obscurity he hadn't realized had turned from a hazy grey to a deep midnight void he hadn't wanted to escape.

Yes, in London he was never alone—there was always a rousing game of cards to be had, or a new ladylove to entertain. But he knew not one of them remembered him past their brief moments together.

Would Pippa remember him now that he was gone?

The thing about being forgettable is that Lucas also forgot those he left behind—or did they leave him behind?

Deep down, he knew he'd never forget Lady Pippa. In the late night hours, or noonday sun, she would be all he thought about, though he would be tied to another.

Christmastide would forever more be a time of loss, much like the frigidly cold nights had been since Randolph was taken from him. Possibly more painful as the years passed and he saw Pippa about London—she would certainly find a good match. She would even fall in love, have children, and live a life many could only dream of.

Not Lucas—he did not allow himself to dream.

But for Pippa, he would have dreamed again. Dreamed of being a better man, a man not weighed down by his past, a man with a heart to give…not an empty shell.

Lucas took heart in knowing that scandal would never touch Pippa—she may not know what he'd given up for her, but he knew. He would marry—dooming himself and, likely, Lady Natalie—to a life without promise, only so it freed Pippa to find all she deserved.

"Maybe it is I who should be leery of the match," his father proclaimed, bringing Lucas back to his current situation. "My son will be a marquis and will have the choice of any young lady he desires."

"Oh, I have certainly heard rumors of how frequently he desires such ladies," Sheridan retorted.

Lucas should take offense to the harsh comment about his rakehell tendencies, but there was no point. At one time, Lucas would have brought his mistress to the opera, or a grand dinner within one of London's most elite homes—and dare anyone to say a negative thing about it to his face. He'd found pleasure in flaunting his scoundrel ways to make sure his parents heard of his antics.

"Besides, you, Bowmont, have no valid causation for withdrawing from the signed marriage contract. It is my family—and my daughter—who are the victims here," Sheridan thundered, his fist slamming against this desk, rattling his ink pot. "My daughter will be scandalized, and her chances of securing a favorable match will decrease exponentially after this mess makes the Post."

"And how will it make the Post?" Lucas spoke for the first time, and both men looked to him as if they'd forgotten he was in the room. "We are all here—your family, my family—I have yet to sign any agreement. And the match was not spoken about in London. There will be no scandal—no lasting shame. I am here, and I am…agreeable—if not happy—with this match."

Both men were shocked into stillness. Lucas didn't bother turning to see his father's reaction. But if Sheridan was any indication of the utter bafflement in the room as his mouth opened and closed much like the small fish

Lucas had used to catch in his family's creek, he knew his father was certainly perplexed.

"Do I need to sign something?" Lucas raised his brow in question. "All of this bickering is unnecessary. As all of London knows, you are partners in many business ventures—very successful ventures, I might add—and it only stands to reason you would both like to keep all the profits within the family. What better way to ensure that than to merge our families?"

Odd that Lucas had never thought much of the way women were used like chattel; traded and bartered in exchange for land, titles, and business. Though, it seemed entirely different when it was a man's life that hung in the balance while awaiting a favorable negotiation and terms.

He understood the reasoning behind the match. They were two very powerful, very wealthy families.

"If we void this contract and end marriage settlement talks, I—and my investment—will walk away from your planned changes in the village," Bowmont said. The victory in his tone told Lucas that his father knew this was his final hand, and it was all he needed to win. "All your hard work would be wasted. Is that what you want, Sheridan?"

"Bloody hell, you know I do not want any such thing!"

"But you are willing to haggle over this marriage settlement all because my son was caught in a storm and sought shelter?" his father asked. "What if he had been lost during the storm—do you know what that would have meant for the future?"

Sheridan remained silent, likely knowing the answer, but also confident Lucas's father was going to remind him.

"I do not have a spare," the marquis said. "After I pass, my estate and title would go to some distant cousin—

including all entailed money I've invested in our business dealings. You would be saddled with a new business partner...and likely, one without my cunning business sense."

Sheridan sighed and shook his head. "Rest assured, you have won. The contract will stand."

"I am no longer satisfied with my family's portion of the contract," Bowmont hissed, knowing he held the upper hand at last. "There are a few things I'd like to amend."

"You are not satisfied with taking my daughter? Now you intend to bleed me dry?"

"I have no such demands..." Bowmont allowed the room to go silent as Sheridan pulled his cravat lose as sweat broke out on his forehead. "I want Lady Natalie's dowry doubled."

"Done," the duke agreed without hesitation, knowing the added dowry did not even begin to skim the surface of his wealth—and overjoyed it was all Lucas's father demanded.

"And the project for the village will start immediately."

"You know that cannot be done," Sheridan said, throwing his arms wide. "It is winter. It is impossible for the villagers to be relocated. We must wait until the coldest weather passes and carriages can be attained to move them."

"Move whom?" Lucas asked, alarmed. "And to where?"

"Until I am deceased, and you take over my estate— Lord help my soul," his father muttered, "that is none of your concern, Maddox."

His father's use of Lucas's honorary title and not his given name was like a slap in the face. He'd refused to address his son directly for years, and now he wanted to deny him knowledge of what Lucas's sacrifices would gain his family. It was unthinkable and worse than being outright ignored.

Lucas had asked a direct question, and his father was attempting to shut him out; going from passive observer to active participant in keeping Lucas at arm's length.

"It is very well my concern." Lucas stood, having taken enough. "Unless you forget, you still need my signature to secure this match. I have reached my majority, and may very well only have a courtesy title at the moment, but I am of an age to make my own decisions."

"And if I cut your funds?" his father asked. "Your lovely townhouse will be gone, your bill at the tailor will not be settled, your cupboards will go bare, and you will have to find another way to support your mistresses."

Previously, all those threats would have had Lucas coming to heel and agreeing to anything his father proposed, but the village? It was the root of Pippa's bleeding heart. He would agree to almost anything to keep her safe, happy, and away from any scandal caused by him or his family. But never would he allow anything to happen to her village.

It would surely ruin her more than he ever could.

"You can take everything I have, but I will not agree to a marriage to Lady Natalie—or any other woman you propose." Lucas moved toward the door, ready to depart.

"If you walk out that door, you will be cut off. Permanently!"

"Then so be it," Lucas retorted. Startled, he realized he was willing to give it all up, no matter if it was only an open threat or idle conversation.

"Where are you going?" Sheridan called in concern. "Bowmont, fix this!"

Lucas halted, turning toward his father. "I am going to save a village and Lady Pippa—something I was unable to do for those dearest to me in my youth."

The door slammed behind him, rattling on its hinges. Besides Pippa's sweet laugh, it was the most satisfying sound Lucas had heard since his childhood. It was something he should have done a long time ago—stood up for himself, not silently begging for his parents to think the best of him.

For a brief moment, Lucas paused, unsure which way would lead him to an exit.

"Lord Maddox." Lady Natalie stood a few paces away, her hand raised, pointing to the right and a long, wide corridor. "The front door is that way."

The girl's porcelain skin was shiny, and blue eyes stared back at him, a hint of sadness showing through, but he sensed the fleeting emotion was not directed at him or his decision. Nevertheless, he owed her an apology for the liberties their parents had taken in arranging a marriage between utter strangers.

He hesitated further, trying to find the right words that would say all he needed to say, but not injure the girl further. "I am sorry our meeting did not go as planned, my lady."

"Your heart is settled elsewhere, I cannot fault you for that." Her arm fell to her side, and her chin lifted in defiance. "No one asked where my heart lies."

"I know it cannot lie with a stranger," he responded, taking a step toward her, begging her to understand, to know he had not meant to injure her in any way, least of all, emotionally. "There will be another, far more suitable man for you."

The girl laughed, a hollow, empty sound—nothing like the carefree, unbridled way Pippa's seemed to escape her without notice. "Do not flatter yourself to think I could love you or feel any affection at all."

Her words were cruel and unnecessary. Their betrothal was not to be, Lucas had signed no papers, nor had their match been known to anyone outside of Somerset. The thought of Pippa calling this girl a friend baffled Lucas. They were entirely at odds with personality.

"Again, my deepest, sincere apologies for this muddled mess our parents have created for us," Lucas said, meaning every word. "I also regret you needing to hear all that transpired within your father's study."

Lady Natalie shrugged off his apology. "This is best for all concerned. Your heart is elsewhere, as is mine. I do hope you and Pippa fare better than me in your future. She is a lovely woman, and deserves much happiness."

"On that, we agree, my lady." The silence between them lengthened as they stared at one another. Could Lady Natalie be thinking of what her future could have held had Lucas not fallen for Pippa first? "Do call on me if you ever need anything, my lady. Your gracious acceptance of our parting ways is very noble."

"I fear the power to aid me does not reside with you." The sadness returned to her eyes, and Lucas truly wished Lady Natalie found her happy ending, as he was determined to do. "But, you should be going if you wish to arrive at Helton House before the storm hits once more. Do treat my friend with love and kindness—something I failed to give her when she needed it most."

Lucas crossed his arm over his chest in promise. "I will give her nothing but love and cherish her every day. I know she will be happy to see you—when you're ready."

"Maybe someday I will have the words to make my amends with Pippa, but for now, you are what is best for her."

"How can you know that?" he asked.

Lady Natalie pondered Lucas's question for only a second before answering. "She was genuinely damaged when she heard of our match. I have not seen such a betrayed look since it was I who wounded her. Now, you must go—before it is too late."

Lucas gave her a quick bow, blessed to have found Pippa, but he also found solace in knowing he hadn't irrevocably harmed Lady Natalie by ending their betrothal before it had officially begun. "Until we meet again, Lady Natalie. Do have faith that the right man will find you."

"And if he already has—and walked away?" She blinked rapidly to hold back her tears.

"Then believe he will right his course and return to you." All this talk of faith and love was new to Lucas, something his family had lacked, even before Randolph was taken; but he would not make this mistake with Pippa. She would know, every moment of every day, how much she was loved.

That was, if she forgave him for lying to her. Or rather, omitting the truth.

Chapter Thirteen

Pippa crowded into the shallow doorway to be out of the wind and removed her glove, pounding her fist on the door before her. When no one answered, she raised her hand again to knock, a bit louder this time to be heard over the storm. She squeezed a bit closer and slipped her exposed hand into her grey muff for added warmth, still clutching her glove.

The storm had returned full force as she'd finished her second delivery in the village, except the temperatures had dropped so severely that heavy snow fell in sheets instead of a drenching rain. The gusting winds brought the snow down in such a way, it blew right into Pippa's eyes. Her nose was too numb to be felt, and her toes ached in her boots. The flakes only lasted a moment before melting and disappearing into her coat.

She should have remained at home—out of the storm—however, she'd needed to escape the confines of that house and fulfill her responsibility to the villagers. No matter how cold she was, Pippa kept in mind that these families needed her. Many ran out of coal long before winter ended. Many were forced to sell off what little they possessed to stay warm, dry, and fed. All the while, the wealthier citizens of England ate extravagant meals each day and spent exorbitant coin on gowns made of satin and lace.

No matter how true it might be, Pippa would not admit she'd continued, despite the growing storm, as a distraction from what broke her heart.

It wasn't that Lady Natalie was to marry, it never had been.

It was that Pippa hadn't found anyone—even with the story of her parent's beginning. She had failed.

Lucas was to wed another, and Pippa felt immense sadness at that fact—an ache so deep and crushing, she doubted it would ever heal and make her whole again. She wanted him to be happy and find contentment—a way to dispel the darkness, just as she wanted her former friend to be happy and well taken care of, no matter how or why their friendship had ended.

But Pippa deserved happiness, too. She wanted more than happiness—she longed for love. A love not always present in societal marriages. What she truly desired was a love and commitment like her parents had…a man willing to endure scandal and ridicule for the woman he loved.

She was being selfish, petty, and entitled. Those were traits that her parents most despised.

Her mind needed to be occupied elsewhere, anywhere, but on the feeling of Lucas's arms around her or his laughter at the sight of her covered in flour in the kitchen or, even, his dour mood and snide comments when he'd first arrived. Yes, Pippa would also look favorably on that moment as well, despite her irritation at his forthright manner.

It was a never-ending cycle that had pounded her senses the entire drive to town as she'd sat alone in her carriage. She was undeniably attracted to Lucas—all of him. Then she remembered his lies, his deception. A sense of betrayal hit her so swiftly, she wondered how she could see past the fury over his dishonesty. With a few beats of her heart, she'd remember the way he'd tried to rescue her shattered angels and, again, Pippa could only remember the light in his eyes that pushed past the darkness that tried to keep him locked within.

Their time together had only impacted her after he was gone.

It was odd—while in the kitchen, she hadn't thought to commit everything to memory; the way he'd moved about the room, the way he'd leaned his hip against the table and crossed one ankle over the other, the way he chuckled as if neither of them had another care in the world, and the way he'd crimped the pie crust and taught her something new. The way he'd lifted her high to re-hang the wreath—allowing her body to slide down his, back to the floor. She'd felt his entire length: his solid chest, muscular thighs, and rigid manhood.

Pippa had wanted more—far more—than she'd received.

Somehow, her mind had known to remember every second of their time together, knowing he would shortly be gone, and the memories would be the only thing left of him.

The door before her swung open with a loud creak. "M'lady," the woman inside called. "Do come in, quickly, afore ye are blown over."

"Thank you, Cassandra," Pippa said, stepping into the thatched-roof house comprised of one room with two large beds and a wood stove in one corner. Not even a table graced the room for meals or schoolwork. Only one candle lit the room. "Merry Christmas. I have brought a gift for Samuel and Lilly—oh, and a pie for you and Hector."

"M'lady." Cassandra curtseyed. Pippa noticed the woman wore nothing but thin stockings on her feet. "Ye did not be having ta do all this, 'specially with a blistery storm brewing again."

"Presents!" Two little heads popped from under the blanket on the straw mattress across the room. "We need presents!"

"Ye two scoundrels be remember'n ye manners," their mother scolded.

"Thank ye, m'lady," the pair chimed in unison.

"Thank *you*, my lady," Pippa corrected with a laugh. "Do not forget the lessons I taught you."

"We will not, my lady," Lilly said, ducking back under the blanket for warmth.

"Make certain you do not, or your mother will send for me, and I will have to return to the village to teach your lessons once again," she threatened.

From the children's muffled laughter beneath their covers, no one thought it was any sort of threat.

Pippa leaned close to Cassandra and whispered, "I've included caps, mittens, and a new book for each."

"Ye be too kind."

"There is never enough kindness, especially during the Christmastide season," Pippa said as she handed the two gifts to the woman. "And for you and Hector, a mincemeat pie for supper—Cook included a loaf of fresh bread, as well."

The woman's eyes grew large at the mention of a hearty meal, especially a feast containing meat, which was difficult to come by during the winter months.

The pie and bread were handed over and set close to the stove for what little warmth it gave. Cassandra embraced Pippa quickly and stepped back, ashamed of her impulse to show her gratitude. "Thank ye so very much, m'lady. We be having a Merry Christmas for certain."

"Everyone deserves a blessed Christmastide." Pippa reached forward and gently squeezed Cassandra's hand. "Briars sends his love, as well."

The woman beamed at the mention of her father, Pippa's butler. "He is well?"

"He is very well and will be here tomorrow to spend the holiday with you and your family." After their meal was prepared, and the Duke and Duchess of Midcrest handed out gifts to all the servants, they were free to return to their families for the night or find their quarters early. "Now, make sure those two little ones keep studying."

"O'course, m'lady," Cassandra nodded, making a show of her actions. "Samuel will never grow ta be a smart business gent like his papa if'n he doesn't study hard."

"Very good," Pippa said with a wink. "I must be going. I have many more packages to deliver."

"Thank ye again, and have a blessed holiday."

"You, too, and tell Hector I sent good tidings and blessed Christmastide wishes." Pippa put her glove on and slipped her hands inside her muff before departing the house into the storm once more—six more stops before she could start the journey home.

Pippa brought her hand to shield her eyes from the heavy snow as she stepped, once more, into the brutal storm. Her next stop was only a few yards down the street at Ms. Tartinston's home. She quickened her steps as she held her satchel close, containing her last mincemeat pie before needing to return to the carriage for more.

Her coachman should be waiting at the end of the street, past Ms. Tartinston's home and on the way to her next stop.

She put one foot in front of the other and navigated the street that had piled quickly with snow as she pushed against the wind. Her hood whipped from her head, allowing the storm to play with the strands of hair that had fallen from their pins. Her teeth chattered, but her fingers began to warm in the shelter of her gloves and muff.

The heavy snow made it nearly impossible to see more than five feet in front of her, and the wind kept most other sounds from reaching her. But Pippa swore she heard hooves not far from her.

Maybe it was Hector traveling home after closing his shop.

Pippa turned toward the street and caught a glimpse of a tall horse with a rider pass, but the rider hadn't seen her huddled against the building.

Her shouted greeting went unheard, as well, lost in the storm.

The storm was growing ever worse. Pippa needed to hurry if all the children were to have their gifts to open on Christmas morning.

She lowered her head, placing one palm against the wooden building for support and kept moving. Her next stop shouldn't be too far now, and Pippa would take more time inside and hope the storm lessened.

"One foot in front of the other and repeat," she chanted. "Almost there."

The wall should give way to Ms. Tartinston's door, however, no such thing occurred. Had she missed it? Certainly not.

Pippa kept moving, refusing to give in to any sort of panic. She'd grown up on these very streets, and she knew the town better than her own manor house. She'd played with the children here in her youth. She'd taught at the local school for three years, and she'd dined at the inn with her parents once a fortnight.

Suddenly, her palm no longer felt the wooden wall, and her foot hit something, causing her to stumble. She threw both of her hands before her, dropping the last pie to be lost in the piling snow as she fell to the ground. Her muff flew from her grasp with the bag holding the pie. The hard-packed dirt walk met her gloved hands, and Pippa felt the rocks rip through the delicate material, scoring her hands.

Every instinct screamed for her to get up, keep moving, forget delivering the last pie, and find her carriage. The ache in her hands and back pushed her to curl into a ball and wait to be found. Someone would come looking for her, but would it be before the cold took over, making her entire body too numb to move?

Pippa needed to get up, find her footing—and locate her carriage.

The wind howled around her as the damp snow seeped through her gown, bringing the coldness to her skin. Her torn gloves were no fight against the growing cold soaking through to her bones.

Kicking her feet, Pippa attempted to untangle her skirts to stand, only to find the snow had mounded over her in the short time since she'd fallen.

Pippa squeezed her eyes shut as her body began to tremble—not from the cold, but from panic. Despite the extreme temperatures, a clammy sweat broke across her forehead.

Her fight against the onset of terror was waning, and Pippa screamed out, her voice, once again tossed around in the storm.

She needed to get up.

She needed to move.

She needed to find the safety of her carriage.

None of those thoughts seemed possible as her hair whipped about her face, all her pins scattering in the snow around her. The day had grown dark as dusk threatened to take over the remaining daylight hours.

If the storm grew too harsh and she failed to return home, her father would come for her…he must. Or her coachman. Where was he? He should be aware she was taking far longer than expected.

She moved to her knees and pushed against the ground to stand, pain shooting through her palms and up her arms. It made her ears ring. Despite it all, she gained her feet and stumbled onward, the heavy snowfall making it impossible to see anything. She shuffled her feet, determined not to stumble again.

Out of nowhere, a light penetrated the falling snow, and she heard, "Pippa!"

For a moment, she thought her mind played tricks on her—she was dreaming she'd heard her name.

Her heart wanted Lucas so much that her subconscious heard his voice calling to her in the storm.

It was certainly a sign it was too late for Pippa—the cold and wind were taking over, demanding she succumb to their deathly call. If she perished with the sound of

Lucas's voice in her mind, then it would not be the worst fate to be had.

Pippa would die happy with the promise of her name on his lips once more.

Chapter Fourteen

Lucas spurred his horse onward, holding the lamp he'd taken from Lady Pippa's coachman high and scanning the storm. The seizing in his chest with each gallop made it hard for him to keep a firm hold on the reins. He'd awaited her return at her carriage for as long as he could, but she hadn't come back, and the storm had grown ever fiercer until even the coachman's pleas for Lucas to stay close while he searched fell on deaf ears.

The woman he loved—shocking as that still was to his own mind—was out there somewhere. She could be lost or hurt or even freezing. Lucas needed to find her, no matter the cost to him. He'd left Lady Natalie's home ill-prepared for the cold that would greet him in the storm. The wind blew right to his skin as if he wore no coat at all, his fingers were numb, and he clamped his teeth shut to stop them from chattering.

He hadn't been able to save Randolph, but he could protect Pippa.

He would find her, even if he had to fight the storm all night. He would rescue her and return her safely to her family.

There was no other option left for Lucas.

He would have nothing left of himself if Pippa were gone. She would take what little remained of him after Randolph's passing with her if Lucas couldn't find her.

How had this woman become such an integral part of him—so much so that he knew he'd perish without her—in such a short time? It was as if they'd known one another for ten lifetimes and not just a matter of days.

If he hadn't been a weak man, he never would have departed her home with his parents and Lady Natalie's family. He'd been foolish to think he'd been saving her from certain scandal by agreeing to wed the Sheridan chit. Or thinking Lady Natalie would have him.

If he ever found Pippa—no, *when* he found her—Lucas would never allow her out of his sight again, no matter what she wanted.

Lucas would demand her coachman's head on a spike if anything untoward happened to Pippa.

"Pippa," Lucas screamed again into the storm. His voice was barely audible to his own ears. There was no possibility if she were out there that she'd hear him call—but he had to do something. Beads of sweat spilled down his forehead even though the temperatures had fallen below freezing. "Pippa!"

Her coachman had pointed Lucas in this direction, telling him she'd planned to stop at five houses along this street. His hope was that she'd sought shelter at one of the homes until the storm passed. However, he knew Pippa well enough to know she'd press onward to deliver all her gifts.

She was mad beyond belief—and beautiful with a kind and compassionate soul that called to his. Or at least what was left of his soul after Randolph had taken half with him when he passed.

Lucas could not allow anything to happen to Pippa…she held his remaining half with her.

Before meeting her, Lucas wouldn't have cared about a building that housed the families of villagers and local servants or a school room. The thought of destroying the building to construct another to store a warehouse full of goods to be sold across England would have sounded like a wise business venture, especially with the growth in rural areas of the land.

But no opportunity to line his pockets with more coins was worth all Pippa would lose. She cared about the villagers—their well-being, their livelihoods, and their future successes.

He would not be the cause of destroying everything she held dear.

"Pippa!" From the pelting snow, he spotted a green coat—the same one the coachman had described to him. He pushed his horse harder, faster through the growing, drifting snow to the glimpse of material.

Panic took a firm hold of him, returning warmth to his numb fingers.

Lucas flew from his horse, his feet hitting the ground at a run to get to her, to assure himself he wasn't seeing things that weren't there. He held the lamp a safe distance away as he wrapped his other arm around her, pulling her to her feet, against him—the snow that had started to cover her clinging to her coat, refusing to let go of her.

"Lucas?" Her words were nothing more than a whisper, pushed through teeth chattering from the cold. "It...cannot...be. You...are with...Natalie."

"Shhhh," he coaxed. "I am here, where I should have been all along."

"But...how...did you...find me?" Her arms wrapped around his waist, and he felt the wetness from her clothes soak into his. "I am...so...cold."

Without another thought, Lucas released the lamp and scooped Pippa into his arms. She would not be able to make it to her carriage on foot.

Lucas glanced around to gain his bearings and sense of direction before he headed toward the waiting carriage. He'd only ridden up and down the one street, but he couldn't remember how many times he'd reached the end and turned around to travel the road again in search of her.

He needed to get her to a warm, dry spot—to banish the cold that had set in. He could not see her face clearly, but he suspected her lips were blue, and her fingertips frozen solid.

Pippa had been found, and it was up to Lucas to save her—and himself.

Settling on a direction, Lucas started off. His steps were solid and sure as he moved through the snowdrifts in search of the carriage, his horse's steps followed closely behind him.

They had to find the carriage—there was no other option.

As Lucas continued on, he saw no signs of shelter. The buildings had disappeared behind the falling snow, obscured from view.

"We are almost there," he reassured her. Pippa's body shook with the cold as she absorbed the little heat his body gave off. "It is right ahead."

Lucas saw nothing but never-ending white before him. But he would not feed into her fear by admitting the storm's void was swallowing them whole.

He would push on, carry her the entire way to her family estate if necessary to save her.

Out of nowhere, an arm shot from his left and grabbed his elbow, pulling him sideways until the remaining lamps hanging from the carriage came into view.

"M'lady be unharmed?" the coachman questioned as he threw a blanket around Lucas's shoulders and pulled the carriage door open, pushing them inside. At Lucas's nod, he slammed the carriage door. "We be home before ye know it."

The carriage dipped as the driver climbed to his seat, preparing to carry them all to safety.

Lucas kneeled on the floor of the carriage and settled Pippa on the seat before him. Her eyes were closed, and her body still trembled from the cold. He removed the blanket from his shoulders and laid it across her, rubbing her arms and legs through the material to warm them.

She was still too cold, and Lucas dreaded that she would not wake, no matter how long he worked to return her warmth.

Chapter Fifteen

"Lucas?" Pippa's eyes fluttered open, straining to focus. She was in her carriage, but she had no idea how she'd gotten there or where Lucas had come from. "You are here."

"I am," he whispered, placing a kiss on her cheek. "I am here, and I will get you home."

"You should be with your family," Pippa muttered through her chattering teeth. "...and Lady Natalie."

Lucas shook his head at her words. "No, Pippa. My place was never with my parents or Lady Natalie."

His words confused her, but she'd promised her mother not long ago that she'd listen. He'd left earlier with them to attend Natalie's family's Christmastide celebration. They were betrothed to one another. He should be there, with his intended, not saving Pippa from her foolhardy errands.

It wasn't right, and it certainly wasn't proper.

"You must return to your family," Pippa chastised him.

"You are the closest thing to family I have left," he confided, confusing her all the more.

While her mind was still hazy, Pippa sensed that she could ask him anything, and if she waited, the moment would pass, and he'd lock his darkness deep inside once more—ending Pippa's chance to dispel it for good. It could be the extreme cold that had her thinking such insane thoughts, but she would not allow the opportunity to slip by.

"What do you mean?" she asked. "Your parents are here in Somerset and wanting you close. I am sure of it." Much like her own parents were surely worried that she hadn't returned home before the storm settled once more.

Darkness clouded his eyes, and Pippa knew she'd asked the right question. It was the question he'd wanted someone to ask him for many years. He opened his mouth to speak but clamped his lips shut once more, forbidding the words to escape.

"Lucas, what do you mean?" Pippa's voice was no longer strained or exiting on a stammer as the warmth of the carriage reached through her damp dress. "I am here, and I am listening."

She saw the resistance flee, and his secrets began to flow forth.

Pippa could do nothing but listen as Lucas told of his brother's heartbreaking death and Lucas's accountability for the tragedy. She gasped when he shared how Randolph's cold, lifeless body had been found by the creek where Lucas had banished imaginary pirates during his long night out. She squeezed his hands when he confessed the alienation and continued dismissal by his parents since that day.

A new path—a far more preferable course—cleared for Pippa as her mother's words sprang to mind, so muddled and unclear before now making more sense than anything she'd heard before.

Her heart shattered into more pieces than her cherished angel collection.

He kept talking until Pippa wasn't sure she could handle any more of his pain. But she allowed him to continue, absorbing his hurt and anguish. The carriage swayed gently in the storm.

"I could not lose you, too," he muttered over and over, his shoulders shaking as he allowed his guard to completely fall—and his tears to flow unrestrained.

"You have not lost me," Pippa confessed, pushing to sit on the seat and facing him where he kneeled before her. Reluctantly, he allowed her to move, the blanket falling to her lap. "Look at me, Lucas."

Pippa's hands rose to cradle his face, and she stared into his eyes as the darkness faded. It did not recede as before to be hidden deep. No, Pippa felt, more than saw, the tenseness and tightness leave Lucas, his demons seeping from his body to leave behind only the light Pippa knew was obscured below the surface.

"I do not know how it happened or when," he spoke again. "But, Lady Pippa Godfrey, I am in love with you. I know this sounds impossible since we've been acquainted such a short time, but I cannot envision my life without you. You've returned a part of my soul I'd feared was gone forever."

Pippa continued to hold his face a mere two inches from hers and listened.

"I know I deceived you. I was not fully honest with you about…" he paused, drawing in a deep breath,

"...anything, really. But that part of me is done. I love you...I am in love with you. Your compassionate, caring, smart, witty nature makes me want to be a better man, a man worthy of you."

She contemplated allowing him to go on, but could not take the growing desperation in his voice.

Pippa leaned in, closing the space between their lips, and kissed him, silencing his words.

She had so much to tell him but resigned herself to allow their kiss to convey her feelings, her needs, and her desires. Their kiss deepened as Lucas's tongue explored her mouth.

Wrapping his arm around her, Lucas shifted to sit on the opposite seat, bringing Pippa with him and settling her on his lap. As he moved her legs to straddle his hips, their lips parted.

"Pippa?" The question in his single word was clear.

"I love you, too," she confessed. "I think I've known since you walked through my front door—all furious and drenched. Long before our kiss."

His brow pulled tight, and Pippa laughed. Any remaining chill left her body as the heat from Lucas took hold.

"We kissed," she said again, but it did not seem to clarify anything for him. "Do you not think this means something?"

"I do not know what that signifies," he said, settling his hands on her hips and placing a kiss just below her ear. "But I am happy that something was working in our favor all this time."

"A Christmas kiss certainly means something...does it not? One does not kiss someone they have no designs on." She leaned into him, allowing him to place a trail of kisses down her neck.

"If it were my choice, we'd be wed before *this* Christmastide, my lady," Lucas said, pulling back.

Pippa moaned, immediately missing the warmth of his lips on her. "Truly? It is I you want and not Lady Natalie?"

"I had never set eyes on the lady before today," he said, giving in and placing his lips to her neck once more. "It is you I want—you I need."

"I am yours, Lucas."

The sway of the carriage ceased, and Pippa knew they'd arrived at her home. She feared the connection between them would also stop, but Lucas did not release her, even after the coachman had opened the door and cleared his throat to gain their attention—and bring to their notice the improper nature of their position.

"I haven't a ring, nor am I asking in the proper way. But, Lady Pippa," he said, staring into her eyes, his longing shining through. "Will you marry me and return the beat of my heart?"

"After all you've shared—your past and the secrets that kept you from being yourself—there is nothing I want more than to be your wife." After all Lucas had lived through, all of his misguided guilt and anguish over his brother's death, and the ability of two parents to completely neglect their remaining son so completely that he'd blamed himself for nearly two decades, he'd survived—banished his darkness to live in the light with her.

"I only have one last question."

Pippa's back stiffened at his words. "What is it?"

"Do you think your mother will accept my help in the kitchen?" he asked. "We have a feast to prepare."

Pippa laughed, shaking off the last of the cold from her time outside. "I think she will love to have you with us for Christmastide...just as much as I."

She leaned in once more and pressed her lips to his, unsure when they'd have another opportunity for a moment of privacy.

"Shall we?" he asked, lifting her from his lap and stepping down from the carriage. She took his proffered hand and stepped onto the snow-covered drive.

She nodded, taking in the look of her family land—a thickening layer of snow concealed the ground for as far as she could see. The limbs of the trees separating her land from Lady Natalie's were heavy with fresh white powder.

Nothing was as she'd expected—but her Christmastide promised to be the most perfect holiday yet.

Epilogue

"Is your mother still irritated at my skill with pie crusts?" Lucas asked as the final door closed behind them, and they started the walk back to their waiting carriage. "It is a natural talent, I swear."

Pippa laughed, her cheeks aching from the continuous laughter that had surrounded her and her new husband for most of the day. "My mother is intelligent enough to know that you convinced Cook to give you lessons over the last year."

"The duchess knows?" Lucas asked, surprised.

Pippa turned a hard stare on him. "Of course, she knows. She knows all that transpires under her roof."

Pippa and her mother had found much laughter in discovering that Lucas had been slipping Cook extra coin for lessons in baking.

"Does she know of our kiss this morning over our breakfast meal?" He stopped walking and turned to Pippa, his brow raised. "What about our intimate moment in the snow-covered garden after supper last night?"

Pippa swatted his arm at his mocking, wide-eyed look as if they were school-aged youths caught kissing when their tutor's back was turned. "Come now, we are married—respectably wed, but I assure you, the entire house is abuzz with talk of our love match."

"I am afraid no one in all of England is removed from word of our love." Lucas winked at her, and they continued walking. "Your father took out a full-page ad in the Post to announce our betrothal. Even my father had to admit he was wrong with pushing me to marry another."

Pippa looked toward their waiting carriage as she thought of all that had changed in the last year. She was wed to a man most worthy, who cherished her for who she was and never sought to change her. He'd even joined her in delivering gifts to the village children, and helped her mother with the mincemeat pies. The weather was mild for Christmas day, but the ground was blanketed in the snow that'd fallen during the night. She was outfitted in a warm, woolen coat with a matching muff—a gift from her new family, the Marquis and Marchioness of Bowmont. Lucas wore a coat of the same color but tailored in a much manlier pattern.

They'd spent many hours discussing their pasts and what they wanted for their *future*—not futures because they planned to share only one.

They'd even received an invitation to join Natalie and her new husband for dinner when they journeyed to London after their holiday with Pippa's parents.

And to think, it had all been made possible because of a love story Pippa was most familiar with…

"After you, Lady Maddox," Lucas said, pulling the carriage door open to reveal a small holly wreath complete with a sprig of mistletoe tied high over the top of the carriage ceiling. "What is all this?"

Pippa didn't believe the astonishment in his tone at the sight of the greenery hung so precariously within her family's carriage.

"Will you deny me a kiss, my lady?" he asked when she didn't immediately step into his waiting embrace. "I do not think we should tempt the Christmastide fates by denying them a kiss."

"I would never dream of denying you—or the fates—anything, my dear lord."

Without another thought, Pippa stepped into her husband's waiting arms, rose to her tiptoes, and placed her lips against his.

Somewhere in the distance, Pippa heard several female sighs—the village women had gathered to watch the Earl of Maddox claim his Christmastide kiss from his new wife.

To learn more about Lady Natalie and her story, please read:

How to Kiss A Rogue, Regency Novella
By Amanda Mariel
Coming November 1, 2016

Other Books By Christina McKnight:

A Lady Forsaken Series
Shunned No More, A Lady Forsaken (Book One)
Forgotten No More, A Lady Forsaken (Book Two)
Scorned Ever More, A Lady Forsaken (Book Three)
Christmas Ever More, A Lady Forsaken (Book Four)
Hidden No More, A Lady Forsaken (Book Five)
Also available in an eBook box set!

Standalone Title
The Siege of Lady Aloria, A de Wolfe Pack Novella
A Kiss At Christmastide, Regency Holiday Novella

Craven House Series
The Thief Steals Her Earl
The Mistress Enchants Her Marquis
The Madame Catches Her Duke
The Gambler Wagers Her Baron

Lady Archer's Creed Series
Theodora
Adeline

About the Author:

Christina McKnight is a book lover turned writer. From a young age, her mother encouraged her to tell her own stories. She's been writing ever since.

Christina enjoys a quiet life in Northern California with her family, her wine, and lots of coffee. Oh, and her books . . . don't forget her books! Most days, she can be found writing, reading, or traveling the great state of California.

Follow her on Twitter: @CMcKnightWriter
Keep up to date on her releases:
www.christinamcknight.com
Like Christina's FB Author page:
ChristinaMcKnightWriter

A Kiss At Christmastide

Author's Notes

Thank you for reading *A Kiss At Christmastide, Regency Novella.*

If you enjoyed *A Kiss At Christmastide*, be sure to write a brief review at
Amazon, Barnes and Noble, or Goodreads.

I'd love to hear from you!
You can contact me at:
Christina@ChristinaMcKnight.com

Or write me at:
P O Box 1017
Patterson, CA 95363

www.ChristinaMcKnight.com
Check out my website for giveaways, book reviews, and information on my upcoming projects, or connect with me through social media at:

Twitter: @CMcKnightWriter
Facebook: www.facebook.com/christinamcknightwriter
Goodreads: www.goodreads.com/ChristinaMcKnight

Sign up for my newsletter here:
http://eepurl.com/VP1rP

There are several people I'd like to thank for staying with me through the emotional journey of writing this book.

To Marc, my amazing boyfriend, who continues to stand by my side through the utter chaos that is my creative process. Thank you…your love and dedication never ceases to amaze me. I hope to one day be as selfless and compassionate as you are.

To Lauren Stewart, my critique partner and best friend, you pushed me to explore new avenues of thought that I never dreamed possible. If we were in a true relationship, it would be one based on co-dependency, but in a good way. My writing would not be what it is without your comments, criticism, suggestions, and guidance.

I'd also like to thank the wonderful women who've supported me in both my writing career and life, including (but not limited to): Debbie Haston, Angie Stanton, Theresa Baer, Roxanne Stellmacher, Laura Cummings, Annalisa Nicole, Dawn Borbon, Suzi Parker, Jennifer Vella, Brandi Johnson, and Latisha Kahn. I know I'm forgetting people…You have all been very patient and wonderfully supportive of my eccentric ways.

A very special thank you to my editor, Scott Moreland, your skill and professionalism surpass all that I expected. Proofreading done by Anja with Hour Glass Editing.

Cover art and wraparound cover design credit to Sweet 'N Spicy Designs.

Finally, thank you for supporting indie authors.

www.ingramcontent.com/pod-product-compliance
Lightning Source LLC
Chambersburg PA
CBHW021100130626
46552CB00005B/2189